ACTION 12 CINEMA

Written and Designed by
Michael K. Ross

First Pass Editing and Layout
Tracy Barnett

Developmental Editing
Caleb Gillombardo

Final Editing
Ian Woodworth

Final Layout
Roo Thompson

Graphic Design
Tom Cantwell

Character & Production Sheets Design
Eden M-W

Cover Art
Brian Patterson

Interior Art
Mike Spivey & Zac Pensol

SPECIAL THANKS

My kids, John-Gabriel and Jacob, whom I love more than anything. Playing games with them brings me more joy than I could ever express in words. But they also keep me humble, because they do not care one iota that I podcast about games, run a gaming convention, or have now written my own game.

My loving wife, Valerie, who has supported me in all my various hobbies and interests despite not 'getting it'. Without her, this book would not exist.

To all my wonderful friends collectively known as the Faculty of The RPG Academy, who support me everyday in so many small and big ways. Specifically, Evan, Caleb, Tom, and Chris - I can never say thank you enough for all the time you gave to me through the podcasts, Faculty retreats, and AcadeCon. Truly, you are amazingly kind and generous.

And a very special thank you to the following people for their early feedback about **Action 12 Cinema** at various playtests. Your laughter at the table inspired me to continue, and your thoughtful feedback helped shape the game's rules to be better and better.

Brian Abels, Asushunamir Arney, Tracy Barnett, Audrey Bedwell, Pete Bunn, Chris Burlew, Tom Cantwell, Angela Curtis, Raevyn Emrick, Jason Flowers, Shannon Fox, Dan Frohlich, Kevin Galli, Caleb Gillombardo, Brandise Grimes, Joseph Homan, Monika Jarvis, Andrew Joines, Trevor Jones, Brad Knipper, John Kromenaker, Elspeth Lambeth, Benjamin Menard, A. Lewanika Miller, Glen Myers, Josh Newton, Chris Nieporte, Mary O'Malley, Jason Oliver, Zac Pensol, David Perrin, Kevin Prehn, Valerie Ross, Alex Rudewicz, Missy Scent, Logan Shen, Gabe Shroyer, Melody Shroyer, Frank Sloan, Andrew Smith, Jared Smith, Kevin Smith, Kenzie Spicer, Danielle Thomas, John Thompson, Mat Thornburg, John Vargo, Michael Waldschlager II.

ACTION 12 CINEMA

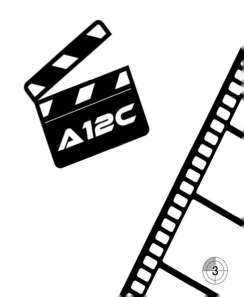

THE PINNACLE OF THE POLYHEDRAL

I believe, with absolute certainty, that the d12 is the Pinnacle of the Polyhedral. To me, it's simply the best die to roll at the table, and as my friend Richard Kreutz-Landry explains, "It's less pointy than a d4. It's more roundy than a d6. It's 100% more regular polyhedronatical than d8s." And who can argue with that?

Sadly, the rest of the TTRPG Community isn't (yet) united behind this belief, and the d12 doesn't get nearly the amount of attention and use it deserves. I set out to change this with my first TTRPG — **MRANOCRLRPG!** — which, of course, stands for "Michael's Ridiculously and Needlessly Overly Complicated Rules Lite Role Playing Game". If it's not already obvious by the name, I began that project as a literal joke. It was a ploy to see how many d12s I could get people to roll at one time while also playing some silly improv games.

As it turned out, playing improv with your friends and rolling a bunch of d12s can be a lot of fun. Time after time, I would wrap up a session of **MRANOCRLRPG!** and people would say, "That was fun!" After the jokiness faded, I was left with the bare bones of an actual (and fun) game. So, I kept tinkering.

The game you now hold in your hands may have manifested out of the ashes of **MRANOCRLRPG!**, but it is a very different game. A much better game, that is still about rolling a bunch of d12s and playing pretend with your friends, but which has been honed down and built back up to tell specific types of stories: B-grade action movie stories. The kind of movies where the bad guys line up to attack the heroes one at a time, or where the hero has to cut a wire on a ticking time bomb – is it the blue one or the green one? The movies where our heroes look on in awe of something so beautiful the budget wouldn't allow for it, so they have the characters describe the alien spacecraft instead of showing it. The type of movies where a hero can throw a bomb just out of frame and it's fine, because the writers couldn't think of a better way to deal with it. This game is all about telling stories like those movies.

Actually, my love of movies — and specifically those types of movies — proved to be the final ingredient that turned **MRANOCRLRPG!** into *Action 12 Cinema*. I am a lover of movies in general, and I grew up watching a lot of B (and, if I'm being honest, a lot of C) grade action movies on my local TBS and WGN stations. I was already using a lot of film language when playing and running more traditional RPGs, so it's a wonder that it took so long to make that final connection.

But thankfully I did, and thanks to the love and support of my friends and family — as well as a bunch of Kickstarter supporters — you can now play pretend and roll a bunch of d12s with *Action 12 Cinema*. Let's play!

WHAT IS ACTION 12 CINEMA?

Action 12 Cinema is a GM-less, rules lite storytelling game that combines dice-generated random elements with player-driven storytelling, improv, and roleplaying, and filters it through the classic three act structure to simulate the experience of B-grade action movies. It's also a game where the players blur the lines between playing characters in the movie and the actors playing those characters, as well as the writers, director, and maybe even the editor or sound mixer of the movie.

In *Action 12 Cinema*, a group of 3 to 6 friends create a story that is one part drama, two parts melodrama, and three parts over-the-top B-grade action movie silliness. When you're finished, you should have a story of epic action that rivals movies like Kull the Conqueror (but not Conan the Barbarian) or Alan Quartermain and the Lost City of Gold (but not Raiders of the Lost Ark) or The Last Starfighter (but certainly not Star Wars — at least, not the good ones). Each session should take roughly four hours, but you can vary the length by changing the number of Obstacles used per Act.

Players use d12 tables to help guide their choices as they collaboratively build the type of movie they want their session to emulate. Next, the players create a couple locations where the game's action takes place, a cast of supporting characters that will fit into the story they're building, and their characters, who will be the Heroes in their B-grade action movie story. Finally, they determine five common Action Movie Tropes that their Heroes can leverage for mechanical effect.

Once that's finished, it's time to begin the story.

Each player introduces their character into the story with a short scene. This scene doesn't require any dice rolls; they just describe how their character is introduced to the audience. Next, the players choose amongst themselves one character to begin Act One by introducing the first Obstacle — the conflict to be resolved in the Act.

Play is broken down into three Acts, with other short scenes between, and culminates in a big action movie spectacle. Players take turns as the Active Player, building and rolling a pool of d12s, with the results determining their progress towards resolving the Obstacle. Play continues until all the Obstacles have been resolved. It's important to understand that an Obstacle can be resolved in a way that shows the Heroes "losing": sometimes the Heroes get captured, and sometimes the bad guys escape.

Action 12 Cinema is different from many traditional RPGs in the breadth of narrative control which the Active Player can assert. The narrative of the game can shift from the Active Player roleplaying as their Hero, to roleplaying as the fictional actor playing that Hero, to the disembodied voice of the director or producer commenting on the actor's performance or the character's actions.

Action 12 Cinema is designed to be a one-shot game, meaning each game you play will likely have unique Heroes, Settings, and Obstacles. While the characters can be carried into sequels — or entire franchises — there are no rules for advancing characters (other than emotional growth and building bonds between characters). They're action movie heroes. They've already got all the skills and abilities they need, and if they don't, they actually do — they just have to find it within themselves. That power was always there all along!

Now, sit back, relax, and enjoy the "So bad, it's good" storytelling of *Action 12 Cinema*.

IS THIS A STORYTELLING GAME, OR A ROLEPLAYING GAME?

Yes!

One of the primary design goals for **Action 12 Cinema** was to make it a GM-less game, meaning there is no one player who is responsible for preparing or facilitating the entire game. To accomplish this, I designed it so all the players at the table would collaborate to fulfill the duties normally delegated to a traditional roleplaying game's Game Master (or "GM").

When you're the Active Player, you have almost absolute authority to narrate and dictate what's going on in the world. You can describe how your character is bypassing the security system, sneaking through the vents, breaking into the computer lab, and taking out the guards. No rolls are needed, no permission is granted by the GM; you narrate the story as you like.

In those moments, it's very much a storytelling game. But it's also an improv game, and all the players at the table should be as involved as possible. Don't hesitate to allow the other players time to roleplay some of the supporting characters or adversaries in the scene. Maybe the scene lingers on the two guards for a few moments before the Active Player's Hero takes them out. Two other players could jump in and roleplay a short scene of the guards in a passive-aggressive argument about whose turn it is to go get coffee, or one of them talking about their coed church league's upcoming softball championship.

If roleplaying random guards isn't your thing, you could bring in additional Heroes during the infiltration. All the players that have their Heroes present in the scene can roleplay doing the super-spy stuff, or maybe one player is the "Person in the Chair", and they're chatting back and forth on comms the whole time.

Ultimately, **Action 12 Cinema** shifts easily between being a storytelling game or a roleplaying game, but it can be either or both, depending on what you want from the game. In some cases the switch between storytelling and roleplaying might occur between individual players, or from scene to scene. Both are excellent ways to play and have a good time. If you're ever unsure if you're doing it correctly, just remember The RPG Academy motto: "If you're having fun, you're doing it right!"

AN EXAMPLE OF PLAY

As a way to help illustrate how the game works at the table, let's take a look at an example of play. Although I take a lot of liberties to help clarify or showcase game elements, this example is heavily based on an actual session that was streamed on the Rook & Rasp Twitch Channel, and can still be viewed on their YouTube channel.

In this example, we have Debra playing Theresa May, a very popular local high school senior. She's best friends with the local slacker, James, who's being played by Oscar. We also have Chad, the local quarterback (and Theresa's ex), played by Sasha. Finally, we have Dell, who works at his father's service station and is a few years older than the other Heroes, played by Mark.

We pick up at the start of Act One, at the service station where Dell works. Our Act One Obstacle is Quicksand, but for this movie we interpreted that as Sinkholes. Theresa May and James arrive in her car to get gas, Dell is working behind the counter, and Chad walks into the store to pick up a drink. The scene begins with some stereotypical high school drama as Chad tries acting 'too cool for school' in front of Theresa May, while James is busy 'shopping' for snacks in the background before heading to the bathroom.

As this is happening, sinkholes are beginning to open up around town, and one of them begins to open up under the service station.

QUICKSAND

Debra: "Theresa May walks outside and finishes pumping gas into the car. The camera pans up to show a sinkhole opening up at the car lot across the street. All of the alarms start going off as cars begin falling into the spreading hole. Theresa can't see this, but she hears all the car alarms and starts looking around. Before she realizes, another sinkhole opens just below her car, and as she removes the gas pump nozzle her car just disappears from view. She stands there, looking where it was for a second like Wile E. Coyote before she falls as well, but she holds onto the gas pump hose so she doesn't fall to her death."

Debra decides that she now wants to roll the dice for her turn. She's described the action so far, how it's affecting her character, and how her character is trying to overcome the Obstacle. In this case, how it's affecting her character vs. trying to stop the sinkholes from forming — either are totally fine.

Debra builds her Dice Pool. She begins with the minimum pool of one d12. She uses her Brawn attribute — which is rated at +1 for her Hero — so she now has two d12s in her Dice Pool. She then decides to use one of her +2 Skills, "Gymnast", explaining that all her training would have given her the incredible grip strength she needs to hold onto the gas pump nozzle, increasing her Dice Pool to four d12s. She doesn't have a Relationship she wants to use here, and she doesn't want to bring in any Tropes just yet, so her Dice Pool for the scene resolves at four d12s.

She rolls a 6, two 8s, and a 12, which count as four Successes, as both 8s are Successes and the 12 is a Heroic Success, which counts as two Successes. Someone at the table marks off those four Successes as progress towards the twelve total Successes needed to resolve the First Act Obstacle of Quicksand (i.e. Sinkholes). Debra decides to keep the 12 for a Heroic High Five later in the game, and ends her turn by narrating:

Debra: "Theresa May screams as she falls, and for a moment the camera continues to shoot a stationary shot on the gas pump, so it looks like she's gone. But after a beat, the camera tilts down and we see Theresa May swinging back and forth at the end of the gas pump hose. She's trying to find footing, but for now she's safe because she's got a death grip on the gas pump nozzle."

Debra ends her turn, and Sasha says she's ready to go next.

Sasha: "Chad pays for his stuff, probably an energy drink and a protein bar, with a crisp $20 and smugly says, 'Keep the change,' to Dell. Just then, the whole building starts to shake. Chad stumbles a bit

and drops his drink and protein bar. The can falls to the ground and starts to roll, picking up speed. It just keeps going faster and faster."

Mark decides to jump in here.

Mark: "It's clear that it's not actually rolling inside the store any longer. They've just got this can on, like, a board, and filmed it rolling down fast to show the floor is uneven, but it's clearly not actually in the store anymore."

Sasha: "Oh, clearly an insert shot. The whole store shakes again, and the floor starts to fall out from under Chad. He leaps and catches hold of the exterior door frame, just as Theresa falls out of sight. We cut to a close up on Chad's face as he slow-mo screams, "NO!!!!!" and reaches out his hand, which still has the protein bar in it, even though we saw him drop it earlier. After a second to collect himself, Chad runs out and tries to pull Theresa up out of the hole."

At this point, Sasha rolls the dice for her Active Player turn. As always, she starts with one d12. She adds two for Chad's +2 Brawn rating, then adds one more for his "Track and Field" Skill. She's now at four dice, and decides to add one more by using Chad's relationship with Theresa. He's not over their break-up yet, and thinks saving her life could help bring them back together.

She rolls her five dice and gets 1, 3, 6, 9, and 11 — two Successes and one Setback, so overall she has one Success.

Sasha: "Chad grabs the gas pump hose line just as it's about to rip free from the pump, and then hand-over-hand pulls Theresa May up and out of the pit."

Because Sasha rolled a 1, she has to Stress an element she used to build the Dice Pool. Mark suggests she Stress Brawn, because maybe he pulled a muscle from the effort of holding onto the hose, but Sasha says she is going to stress the Relationship instead.

Sasha: "When Chad pulls her up, he says, 'I'd never let you fall like I fell when you dumped me,' and it's clearly a dumb thing to say, so despite saving Theresa May he actually made things worse."

Sasha's turn is now over, and Oscar says he wants to go next.

Oscar: "So this whole time, James has been in the bathroom, drinking a beer he stole from the gas station while sitting on the toilet and looking at a girly magazine. You know, the kind you used to only get at the gas stations?"

Everyone nods.

Oscar: "Okay, so he finishes his business, but when he goes to flush the toilet it actually falls out of sight. He's mostly unphased and just says, 'Wow, that's weird.' He turns to wash his hands, but when he turns on the faucet the whole sink also collapses into the hole. He steps back and almost falls into the hole where the toilet was, but barely avoids it and says, 'This place is a dump.'"

Mark: "Does James sound like Shaggy?"

Oscar: "Absolutely. Now, James opens the door, and everything within a few feet on the other side of the door is just gone. Then the space behind him is also just gone. Pretty much the only thing still standing is the door frame he's standing in, and it's not going to last much longer.

"James can see Chad and Theresa May out by the gas pumps. With a casual stoner grace, James holds onto the top of the door, swings out while he's holding on, and then leaps over to solid ground."

Oscar builds his Dice Pool. He gets the one starting d12, then adds two for his Moxie, because this is a dumb idea and Heroes with dumb ideas thrive on a good Moxie score. He then adds two more for his "I Skate Through Life" Skill, and rolls five dice. He gets two Successes, and the rest blanks.

Oscar finishes up his turn, saying, "James makes it to the gas pumps and starts to say, "You guys won't believe what happened in the bathroom..." but then suggests Mark start his turn before James finishes his story.

Mark: "You hear a revving engine from inside the garage portion of the gas station. One of the bay doors starts to roll up, but then gets jammed because the whole building has shifted a bit, so we see this beat-up pickup truck come bursting out through the garage door with Dell at the wheel. He swerves around the sinkholes and dodges new ones just forming." Mark mimes twisting the steering wheel wildly back and forth which, if it was really happening, would certainly cause him to wreck, but this isn't that sort of movie. "Dell pulls up opposite the trio and tells them to jump in."

All the other players agree that their Heroes climb in the truck — which makes sense — but the players have to agree, since technically Mark is controlling their characters during his turn.

He builds his Dice Pool, starting with one and adding two for his Brains. He also adds two for his "If It Has Wheels, I Can Drive It" Skill. That puts him at five, but he also wants to use his Achilles' Heel of "I'll Do Anything to Impress Theresa May" and, with those two bonus dice, he now has a Dice Pool of seven dice.

He rolls and gets three Successes with an 8 and 12 (12's are called a Heroic Success and count as two successes), and a 1. Since he used his Achilles' Heel, the 1 counts as two Setbacks instead of one, completely canceling the two Successes given by the Heroic Success and leaving him with a net total of one Success. He also still takes the Stress from the Setback, which he must apply to one of the elements he used to build his Dice Pool. He chooses to apply it to his "If It Has Wheels, I Can Drive It" Skill — Mark's truck took some damage going through the garage door.

Mark: "Everyone scrambles into the bed of the pickup and he drives off, outrunning the spreading sinkholes. A drone shot with terrible CGI shows that the entire town is a smoking ruin."

At this point, the players decide to transition to another scene where they are riding in the truck and listening to the radio, trying to find out what's going on. Since they haven't yet gotten to 12 total Successes, the Act One Obstacle (Sinkholes) is still active, and they discuss how they think their Heroes would try to overcome it, or further interact with it.

And that's how one round of **Action 12 Cinema** plays out. Each player takes a turn setting or resetting the scene: what it looks like, what camera angles are being used, how the producer would tweak it, or how certain special effects might look when added in post can happen at any time. The players describe how they are interacting with the current Obstacle or aiding someone else, and then they roll their dice. They then see how many Successes they have, if any, and narrate what that dice result looks like. If someone rolls really badly, things can get worse, and they'd narrate how that happens or how it looks. Until the Complete Success is rolled, these are all Incremental Successes; the main Obstacle is still active, but the Heroes are making progress toward overcoming it — or, at least, trying to keep ahead of it.

For more examples of gameplay, refer to the section "Additional Resources" at the end of the book to see a list of actual play videos and podcasts.

ACTION 12 CINEMA'S CORE VALUES

The Active Player has almost unlimited narrative control. The limitations on the Active Player's control can be summed up with these three Core Values:

1. Maintain the established fiction.
2. Respect the other players' agency.
3. The Active Player decides what happens; the dice determine when and if an Obstacle is resolved.

Unless there is a good and specific reason to make an exception, these Core Values should be followed at all times.

MAINTAIN THE ESTABLISHED FICTION

If an Active Player establishes that the Moon is crashing into the Earth (likely as part of an Obstacle, but hey — maybe that was just a background detail), then another Active Player shouldn't change or undo that fiction on future turns without cause.

Once something has been established as true, it should remain true unless it gets changed or corrected through the mechanics of the game. If the Moon crashing into the Earth is an Obstacle, then it's fine for a future Active Player to narrate how things are working toward changing that; that's all part of the game. The established fiction shouldn't be altered without a compelling narrative reason.

Sometimes these things can happen accidentally. One player says it's night time, and the next player forgets and describes their turn — which is happening about the same time — as a day scene. For examples like this, it's possible to just lean into the Tropes of bad (but fun!) action movies: the time difference was likely due to a missing scene, poor editing, or an attempt to hide a flimsy SFX budget. Those incidents of fiction breaking are fine, fun, and appropriate, as long as everyone is on-board.

RESPECT THE OTHER PLAYERS' AGENCY

If an Active Player wants to include another player's Hero in a scene, they need to get permission first. It would not be fitting for the Active Player to decide that another player's Hero walks into a bar and is quickly taken hostage so that their Hero can rescue them. All that MIGHT be fine, but check with the other player before narrating their Hero in this way. Maybe that player has an idea of their Hero that doesn't mesh with them being taken unaware so easily, or maybe they think this is great. The point isn't to avoid using the other Heroes, but to check with their players before doing so. When playing with someone else's toys, it's always best to ask permission first.

THE ACTIVE PLAYER DECIDES WHAT HAPPENS; THE DICE DETERMINE WHEN AND IF AN OBSTACLE IS RESOLVED

This gets to the heart of how *Action 12 Cinema*'s Obstacle resolution works. When the Active Player narrates a scene, any actions or events they describe happen, but it's unclear whether those actions helped resolve the scene's Obstacle until the dice have been rolled. And just because an action helps resolve the Obstacle, it doesn't necessarily give the Heroes any real advantage. Resolving an Obstacle doesn't always mean the Heroes won in some way; it is possible to resolve an Obstacle and have the Heroes in a worse position than when they started.

To reference an earlier example, the Active Player describes their character breaking into a high security complex, navigating the air vents, taking out the guards, and then hacking a mainframe. If the current Obstacle is to break into a High Security Complex, the Active Player can SAY they did all of those things, but if the dice don't generate enough successes to resolve that Obstacle, then

KISSUS INTERRUPTUS

the Obstacle is mechanically still ongoing. The players then get to determine why the Obstacle has not yet been resolved, like a sort of story logic puzzle.

Perhaps they only manage to get through the first layer of security and must now find their way deeper into the facility, or their hacking has alerted security and now killer robots are approaching their location while the program is working, complete with a progress bar as the camera cuts between the Hero and the killer robots attempting to break in and atomize them. Although technically still within the Obstacle of breaking into the facility, the perspective has shifted, and now they're fighting killer robots.

Another very important factor is that there is no narrative weight built into how an Active Player chooses to attempt something. If they want to try and fight the Space Vampires with their laser rifle — cool! If they want to challenge their leader to a dance off, with the Earth as the prize for the winner, that's equally as cool. The game makes no distinction whether any of the players' actions make more or less sense than any other. Players still build a Dice Pool the same way, and Successes move the story closer to resolving an Obstacle. If a Vampire Dance Battle gets enough Successes to end the Space Vampire threat, then it works!

Understanding how the Active Player's agency works is a big part of understanding how to play **Action 12 Cinema**, and how to get the most fun out of it. There are more examples later in the book, but this should clarify the broader strokes of overall gameplay.

HOW TO PLAY

Each session of **Action 12 Cinema** occurs in two distinct phases: the Pre-Production Phase and the Production Phase.

PRE-PRODUCTION PHASE

The Pre-Production Phase is when the players plan out the film they'll be playing. This phase usually takes about an hour and a half with new players, but returning players can usually complete this phase more quickly.

- Everyone gets a Character Sheet and their own copy of the Production Sheet
- Set the Rating and cover Safety Tools
- Choose Genre and Set Era(s)
- Choose the BBEG
- Choose the Plot
- Choose the six primary Obstacles, and place them in the order they will be introduced (one in Act One, two in Act Two, three in Act Three)
- Create the Opening Scene and Final Stage Locations
- Create the starting Supporting Characters
- Create the Heroes
- Determine the starting Tropes

PRODUCTION PHASE

The Production Phase is when the players make the movie magic happen. This phase usually takes about three hours when using the standard Three Act playstyle.

- Character Introduction scenes
- Act One The Inciting Incident
- Interstitial Scene as needed/wanted
- Act Two The Rising Tension
- Interstitial Scene as needed/wanted
- Act Three The Final Showdown
- Concluding Scenes
- Name the Movie
- Post-Credits Stinger (optional)
- Post Game Discussion/Wrap-up

ACTION 12 CINEMA
- Production Sheet -

RATING	GENRE	ERA	BBEG	PLOT

LINES:

VEILS:

LOCATIONS

Start:

Finale:

SUPPORTING CAST

MAIN CAST

OBSTACLES	ACT 1	ACT 2	ACT 3

ACT 1 TROPES	ACT 2 TROPES	ACT 3 TROPES

THE PRE-PRODUCTION PHASE IN DETAIL

One player assumes the role of the Facilitator and guides the players through these Pre-Production steps. As story elements are chosen they are added to the Production Sheet, to be used as a reference to keep the story cohesive through the Production Phase. It may be better to have one digital copy everyone can reference in an online game, but for in-person games it's better for everyone to have their own sheet.

SET THE RATING

By default, **Action 12 Cinema** stories are rated PG-13. This generally means there will be limited drug use, brief non-sexual nudity, and some non-sexualized adult language (you have one F-bomb — use it wisely). Violence will not be graphic or gory. Children may be put in danger, but no individual child will be seriously harmed, and the dog will likely survive, as well.

As a group, the players should come to an agreement on whether the rating of the game will fall into the standard PG-13 or something else (Generally G, PG, PG-13, R, or NC-17). The goal is to make sure everyone is comfortable with the rating, and will have fun during the game.

Find full explanations of what each Rating means here:
https://www.motionpictures.org/film-ratings

SAFETY TOOLS

Even when everyone is on board with whatever-rated game, the use of safety tools is strongly recommended before and during any **Action 12 Cinema** game. There are lots of various safety tools available, but the minimum recommended tools are Lines and Veils and the X-Card.

LINES AND VEILS

Lines and Veils are established boundaries for the story, and are defined by each player individually. Generally, they are shared with the table before the start of a game or campaign.

Lines are hard boundaries that exclude specific content from the game in any form or fashion. For example, if a player chooses non-consensual sex as a Line, then non-consensual sex will not be depicted — or even referenced — during the game.

Veils are softer limits where the player is okay with the themes or depictions being included in the game, as long as they are not being explicitly described. Content specified as a Veil will be hand-waved without going into detail, or might even happen off-screen.

For example, a player may have chosen consensual sex as a Veil. During play, a Hero may want to seduce a hapless security guard to further the plot. That's totally fine, but there's no need to spend any table time on it. The Active Player can describe the characters involved going into a bedroom and closing the door, then it's a hard cut to the next morning. Our Hero walks out, looking slightly disheveled and carrying the guard's security badge.

You can learn more about Lines and Veils, compiled by Robert Ian Shepard, at
http://tinyurl.com/lines-veils-rpg

THE X-CARD

The X-Card is one of the simplest safety tools, and it works great in conjunction with Lines and Veils. If someone didn't realize a particular topic would be a Line or Veil for them, but begins to feel uncomfortable during play, the X-Card can be used to immediately end the scene that is causing the discomfort.

A card with a large "X" is placed on the table where everyone can reach it. If anyone feels uncomfortable with something in the game, they simply touch the X-Card. The Active Player should then change the scene immediately by skipping ahead or changing what is happening. The person who activated the X-Card is not expected to explain their reasons.

It's fine if the use of the X-Card causes some plot holes, or makes the story harder to understand. It's a B-Grade movie after all — plot holes and logical inconsistencies are kind of expected.

You can read more about the X-Card, developed by John Stavropoulos, at
http://tinyurl.com/x-card-rpg

RANDOM TABLES

The following d12 tables contain elements to help the players build out their story world. All of the tables are purely inspirational – the players never have to accept a result just because the corresponding number came up on a die. If a particular result doesn't feel fun, or doesn't seem to fit in with the rest of the elements already established, feel free to ignore it – re-roll, choose a replacement, or make up your own. If there is ever a disagreement as to whether or not a random element should be kept, the player who rolled the die has final say.

CHOOSE THE GENRE

By default, **Action 12 Cinema** is about playing "Pure Action" movies. These are very straightforward action movies that lack any heavy genre flavor. Die Hard is an Pure Action movie (but also a perfect movie, so it's not a great touchstone for the types of movies emulated by **Action 12 Cinema**). Any late 80s or early 90s action movie with Arnold Schwarzenegger or Sylvester Stallone is likely an Pure Action movie.

The players should discuss and decide as a group if their session will be played as an Pure Action movie, or if they'd like to add a genre or a mashup of genres. Each genre has its own conventions and tropes, and it's important for the players to establish at least a general idea of the movie's genre before continuing.

D12	GENRE	D12	GENRE
1	+ Adventure	7	+ Sci-Fi
2	+ Creature Feature	8	+ Space
3	+ Disaster	9	+ Superhero
4	+ Fantasy	10	+ Thriller
5	+ Horror	11	+ Western
6	+ Martial Arts	12	Mashup (roll twice)

GENRE DEFINITIONS AND EXAMPLES
Action-Adventure: These films feature "faraway" and "exotic" lands, where the villains and the action become unpredictable.

- Alain Quartermain and the Lost City of Gold
- Big Trouble in Little China
- Romancing the Stone

Action-Creature Feature: These films feature a monster from somewhere else (the deep ocean, another time, outer space), a small town dealing with the emerging threat, and a scientist at the heart of the action.

- Humanoids from the Deep
- Piranha
- Them!

Action-Disaster: The main conflict of this genre is some sort of natural or artificial disaster, such as floods, earthquakes, hurricanes, volcanoes, pandemics, or Kaiju. These films often incorporate elements from the Thriller or Science Fiction genres.

- Armageddon
- King Kong vs. Godzilla
- The Core
- The Poseidon Adventure

Action-Fantasy: This genre is similar to Action Adventure, but the locales are often magical lands and feature magic and monsters. The protagonists typically come from a common birth and rise to prominence through their actions.

- Labyrinth
- Masters of the Universe
- The Beastmaster

Action-Horror: This genre combines the intensity of a horror film with the fighting or brutality of an action film.

- Fright Night
- Pitch Black
- The Predator
- The Thing

Action-Martial Arts: This genre focuses on hand-to-hand combat scenes between characters, using martial arts as the primary method of storytelling and the vehicle for character expression and development.

- Best of the Best
- Bloodsport
- The Last Dragon

Action-Sci-Fi: This genre weaves science fiction elements into action film premises, and often emphasizes gun-play, space battles, and super soldiers.

- Face/Off
- I Come in Peace
- Universal Soldier

Action-Space: This genre's films are, as suggested, action movies set in space. They usually contain science fiction elements, and can include elements of nearly any other genre.

- Enemy Mine
- Robinson Crusoe on Mars
- The Last Starfighter

Action-Superhero: This genre focuses on one or more individuals who possess superhuman abilities. They often have science fiction or fantasy elements, and usually deal with the origins of a character's special powers and their first confrontation with their nemesis, who often also possesses superhuman abilities.

- Dark Man
- The Phantom
- The Shadow

Action-Thriller: This genre focuses on fast pacing and high stakes. They tend to feature big explosions, lots of violence, and a clear – often flamboyantly evil – antagonist.

- Con Air
- Firestarter
- Road House

Action-Western: This genre is set in the American West, and embodies the spirit, struggle, and demise of the new frontier.

- The Quick and the Dead
- Tombstone
- Young Guns

WHAT ERA(S)?

Once the genre has been chosen, determine the era or time frame for the action movie's setting. There is no chart for this – just a quick group discussion. Is the Pure Action movie set as an 80s movie, a 90s movie, or in the present day? Is the Action Western movie set in the 1800s, like Tombstone, or in the distant future, like Mad Max?

The time period of the film's production can also be determined here. Perhaps the story revolves around an Action Sci-Fi film set in the year 2587, but the movie is being made in the 1960s and has that level of production design and special effects. By changing the movie's production era, the story's tone can be shaped by that time period's technology, aesthetics, and current events.

Please be kind and thoughtful while playing **Action 12 Cinema**. As someone who loves action movies – I mean, I really love 'em, warts and all – there is no need to keep the sometimes casual, and all-too-often blatant, racism and sexism inherent in many of these films. While **Action 12 Cinema** is a love letter to action films, it's entirely possible and proper to pick out and keep the parts we love, and trash the parts we don't.

There's no place for problematic tropes at the table while you're playing **Action 12 Cinema**. Even if you're playing an Action Western movie that you've set as being made in the 1950s, you shouldn't lean into the racist depictions of Native Americans that were common in these films at that time. Same with any other marginalized group; everyone is welcome at our tables, and everyone should be comfortable at our tables. Using some common courtesy, as well as the suggested safety tools (or others you may want to use instead), should keep everyone's focus on the over-the-top action silliness – where it belongs – and away from cruel and outdated views on women, people of color, and any other marginalized group.

WHO IS THE BBEG?

BBEG is TV/movie terminology for Big Bad Evil Guy/Girl/Person. Who, or what, is pulling the strings? Scheming schemes? Master-minding?

Now that the genre and era have been established, the players choose the antagonist for their film. Choose from one of the tables below, or roll two d12s; the first die determines which table to use, while the second determines the result on that table.

As with all the random elements in **Action 12 Cinema**, you may need to do some creative thinking to find a way to fit a rolled BBEG into your story. Some can be used literally, like 'Werewolf', while others might need a bit of interpretation, like 'Fate' or 'Secret Society.'

If there's fun to be had smoothing the corners off some odd combinations, go for it. If not, re-roll or choose a better option for your session. All these random elements should be used to make the game fun and not hinder the story.

1-3: BBEG CHART #1

D12	GENRE
1	Environmental/Natural Disaster
2	Zombies
3	Vampires
4	Aliens
5	Kaiju
6	Cult
7	Pirates
8	Terrorists
9	Mad Scientists
10	Evil Corporation
11	Secret Society
12	Robots

4-6: BBEG CHART #2

D12	GENRE
1	Ninja
2	Tyrannical Government
3	Monster
4	Fascists
5	Super Villain(s)
6	Clones
7	Sasquatch
8	Werewolf
9	Ghosts
10	Wraiths
11	Demon/Demonic Forces
12	Giant Animals

7-9: BBEG CHART #3

D12	GENRE
1	Mummy
2	Scarecrow
3	Dragon
4	Goblins
5	Fey
6	Wizard
7	Hackers
8	Evil Rich Person/ People
9	Cosmic Horror
10	Religious Institution
11	Fanatic
12	Table's Choice

10-12: BBEG CHART #4

D12	GENRE
1	Fate
2	Mythological Creatures
3	Nightmares Come to Life
4	Corrupt Politician
5	Lich/Undead Sorcerer
6	Shapeshifters/ Dopplegangers
7	Super Villain(s)
8	Yourself from the Future
9	Cosmic Horrors
10	Sentient A.I.
11	Roll Twice and Combine
12	Table's Choice

THE PAPER THIN PLOT

The movie needs a plot, no matter how paper thin it is… right?

Now that the antagonist has been determined, the players choose the Plot of their movie, or roll two d12s, with the first die determining the table used, and the second die determining the result from that table.

1-2: MOVIE PLOT TABLE 1

D12	GENRE
1	Propaganda Film (Needs to be Made/Stopped)
2	Trying to Harness the Power of Ancient Sites
3	Build a Secret Base
4	Clone/Replace World Leaders
5	Hold the World Hostage
6	Expose the Truth about Aliens
7	Blackmail
8	Discover/Protect/Loot Ancient Location (i.e. Atlantis)
9	Build Killer Robots
10	Open Wormhole
11	Control the Weather
12	Create Earthquakes

GOVERNMENT AGENCY OF FICTION

3-4: MOVIE PLOT TABLE 2

D12	GENRE
1	Asteroid
2	Meteorite
3	Control of Satellites
4	Control of Radio Waves
5	Open Dimensional Portals
6	Create Super Soldiers
7	Create Super Weapons
8	Use Time as a Weapon
9	Use the Necronomicon
10	Escape
11	Assassination
12	Oppress the Weak

5-6: MOVIE PLOT TABLE 3

D12	GENRE
1	Civilians Need Help Against an Overwhelming Force
2	Corruption in an Organization Meant to be Helpful
3	REVENGE!
4	Race Against the Fascists
5	Subliminal Messages to Control the Populace
6	Technology Used for Evil
7	Blackmail
8	Opposing Forces After the Same Goal
9	Overthrow Tyranny
10	Entity Wants to Devolve Humans
11	Element + Animal (i.e. Sharknado or Lavalantula)
12	Outside Entity Invades Earth

7-8: MOVIE PLOT TABLE 4

D12	GENRE
1	Entity Transforming Humans
2	Alien Invasion
3	Flood the Planet by Melting the Glaciers
4	Shrinking
5	Trapped in Another Universe
6	Massive Earthquakes
7	Sickness from Another Place/Time/Dimension
8	Traitor on the Inside
9	Sinking Boat
10	Destroy All Humans!
11	Time Crimes
12	Player's Choice

9-10: MOVIE PLOT TABLE 5

D12	GENRE
1	Break Into a Vault
2	Holding Earth's Oxygen Hostage
3	Living Nightmares
4	Cosmic Rays
5	Prison Break
6	Moon Crashing into Earth
7	Former Student Returns to Their School for Revenge
8	Old Rich Dude Trying to Scare People by Pretending to be a Monster/Ghost
9	Can't Escape Fate
10	Mythological Beings are Real and Here Now.
11	Escape Hostile Place or Environment
12	Got to the Deadly Place and Bring Someone or Something Back Out

11-12: MOVIE PLOT TABLE 6

D12	GENRE
1	Someone/Something Knows What You Did
2	Mistaken Identity
3	Monster with a Personal Grudge
4	Transported to a Magical World
5	Keep the Mystical McGuffin from the Bad Guys
6	Pulled Back In to the World You Left Behind
7	You're the Innocent Patsy. No One Told Them You're Also a Badass.
8	Escape to Prove Your Innocence
9	Far from Safety, in a Damaged Vessel
10	Your Wildest Dreams Came True. It's a Disaster.
11	Roll Twice and Combine
12	Table's Choice

As with the tables for the BBEG, the entries for the Plot tables are open to interpretation. They should be coaxed to fit the narrative the players are creating. If the Plot from the table doesn't work, simply re-roll on the table or choose an option which works for the narrative.

LAYING OUT THE ACTION BEATS

A standard game has six Obstacles: one for the Inciting Incident in Act One, two for the rising tension in Act Two, and three in the Final Showdown and resolution of Act Three. Use the tables below to randomly generate all six of these now, or choose or make up your own, and decide in what order they'll be introduced.

In earlier versions of **Action 12 Cinema**, we waited until the Locations, Supporting Characters, and Heroes were created before we determined our inciting incident. But it became apparent during the play tests that having the knowledge of what the Inciting Incident was going to be helped the players create Locations, Supporting Characters, and Heroes that fit better and made for a more cohesive story, so, by default, I now have this part happening here. If you want a more chaotic experience, feel free to wait until it's time to introduce the Inciting Incident (or any of the Obstacles) to determine what it is and introduce it in real time.

1-3: OBSTACLE TABLE 1

D12	GENRE
1	Computer System Failure
2	Quicksand
3	Fight!
4	Space Time Breach
5	Ticking Clock/Bomb
6	Gather Your Resources
7	Fight!
8	Equipment Malfunction
9	Chase
10	Pirates
11	Magical/Technological Defenses
12	Choose Your Own

7-9: OBSTACLE TABLE 3

D12	GENRE
1	Mummy
2	Scarecrow
3	Dragon
4	Goblins
5	Fey
6	Wizard
7	Hackers
8	Evil Rich Person/People
9	Cosmic Horror
10	Religious Institution
11	Fanatic
12	Table's Choice

4-6: OBSTACLE TABLE 2

D12	GENRE
1	Gravitational Anomaly
2	Monsters
3	Fight!
4	Collect all the Pieces
5	Someone/Something Must be Found
6	The Weather is Out of Control
7	Fight!
8	Biological Contamination
9	Everyone is Looking for You
10	Normal Mode of Travel is Now Unsafe
11	"Something" is Unstable
12	Choose Your Own

10-12: OBSTACLE TABLE 4

D12	GENRE
1	Break Into a Place
2	Discover the Weakness
3	Build the Thing
4	Fight!
5	Training for a Specific Foe
6	Fortify the Lair
7	Find a Place to Hide
8	Trace the Source
9	Fight!
10	A Moment of Self-Doubt
11	The Missing Link
12	Choose Your Own

By their nature, these Obstacles are the most generic of all the random elements, and as such they can be applied to a wide variety of circumstances. In many cases, a specific Obstacle can have multiple interpretations, depending on the other elements of the story, such as genre and the other Obstacles surrounding it. An Obstacle can also change form during play; for example, if the Obstacle is "Find a Place to Hide", the Active Player may have to Fight! something already in the hiding place. As long as it makes any sense, it makes enough sense for this B-Grade movie.

AMBUSH
- Heroes being attacked without warning
- Heroes attacking an enemy with planning

A MOMENT OF SELF-DOUBT
- A montage scene where each Hero is given a quiet moment to reflect on what they are about to face and gather their resolve on how they are ready to face it, whatever comes. This is a special Obstacle which can be resolved with narration, rather than rolls.

A MYSTERY TO BE SOLVED
- Find the Killer's identity
- Where is the Money?
- Who is the Double Agent?
- How to get past the traps to find the treasure?

BIOLOGICAL CONTAMINATION
- Super virus escapes a lab
- Virus that turns people into monsters
- Mutagen turns animals into anthropomorphic martial artists
- Alien species grant certain people superpowers
- Alien life form escapes containment
- Food stores ruined by diseases

BREAK INTO A PLACE
- Reverse Prison break
- Get into a high-security lab/complex/government building
- Rob a casino in the Zombie Plague zone
- Get the phone that was confiscated by the school principal

BUILD THE THING
- Gather and Build a machine/vehicle/robot
- Build a super-computer

CHASE
- Heroes are being chased, or are chasing someone/something else. Could be through an abandoned building, city streets, hyper-drive lanes.

COLLECT ALL THE PIECES
- Assemble the Team
- Find the missing sections of the Rod of Six and a Half Pieces
- Investigate a mystery

COMPUTER SYSTEM FAILURE
- Airplane's systems malfunction causing it to crash
- Nuclear reactor approaching meltdown
- A.I. going rogue
- Spacecraft's life support systems failing
- Warp drive malfunctions, dropping a spacecraft into someplace dangerous

DIABOLICAL AND OVERLY ELABORATE DEATH TRAP
- Slowly being lowered into a shark tank
- Narrow walkway dissolving into a vat of acid.
- Laser inching toward restrained captive

DISCOVER THE WEAKNESS
- Test monsters in a lab
- Probe the defenses of an enemy
- Read old books in a secret library

ENDANGERED/INJURED CIVILIANS
- War
- Biological attack
- Monster attack
- Natural disaster
- Building collapses

ENVIRONMENTAL DANGER
- Earthquake
- Avalanche
- Lighting storm
- Inhospitable planet's atmosphere
- Radiation

EQUIPMENT MALFUNCTION
- Government experimenting with alien technology
- Vehicle stalls/crashes
- Millenia-old magical defenses beginning to fail
- Hijacked weather satellites create severe weather

EVERYONE IS LOOKING FOR YOU
- Every assassin in the world knows your name, and there's a $20 million bounty
- Every screen and billboard bears the Hero's face, and a reward

FIGHT!
- Heroes need to assault an island fortress
- Creature feature fight with the monster
- Street fight with ninja
- Zombies attack
- Kaiju attacking the city or each other

FIND A PLACE TO HIDE
- Outrun the assassins, taking them out as you go
- Evade foes with high-tech scanners
- Locate a hidden base you can use to plan your next move

FORTIFYING THE LAIR
- Set traps against an oncoming assault
- Get your weapons together
- Often a montage scene (and a great time for a Needle Drop)

GATHER YOUR RESOURCES
- Assemble the team
- Outfit the team with special gear
- Often a montage scene (and a great time for a Needle Drop)

GRAVITATIONAL ANOMALY
- Gravity too high, or too low
- Super miniature black holes form, causing things to crush into singularities
- Gravity distortions allow limited flight
- Moon being pulled toward Earth

MAGICAL/TECHNOLOGICAL DEFENSES
- Magical barrier to keep intruders out
- Near sentient A.I. Robots patrolling
- A fence, perhaps electrified
- Multiple guard-posts surrounding a crashed UFO
- A narrow bridge that can only be crossed in a specific pattern on glowing rune tiles

MONSTERS
- Vampires
- Werewolves
- Mythological monsters
- Cryptids
- Humanoids from the deep

NORMAL MODE OF TRAVEL IS NOW UNSAFE
- A bridge has collapsed, and you have to find another way across
- An 87 car pile-up in a tunnel means you have to pass through on foot
- Forced to swim through the flooded hallways of an underwater facility
- Emergency lock-down on a space station that requires a spacewalk to by-pass

PIRATES
- Space Pirates
- Modern-day pirates
- Fantasy world pirates
- Time pirates
- High School Rival is the Pirates, and now they're zombies attacking your school

PLAN IT OUT
- Often a montage scene of how the next step will go (though it rarely does)

QUICKSAND
- Actual quicksand
- Any situation where the Earth could open up beneath the Heroes' feet
- A skyscraper being shrunk with people inside, who must escape before it traps and kills them
- Sinkholes are opening up around a small town

CONCERT CLIMAX

"Alas, poor Yori---" *BOOM!* — Enter Rex + A-Bomb-inable Snowman

RADIATION
- Nuclear fallout
- Alien radiation seeping through a wormhole
- Time loops caused by spatial collapse
- Alien technology causing sleep deprivation

"SOMETHING" IS UNSTABLE
- Gravimetric anomaly
- Time warp
- Wormhole
- Building collapsing
- Paranoia causing a small workforce to turn against one another

SOMEONE OR SOMETHING MUST BE FOUND
- Find a missing person
- Find the final clue and locate the McGuffin
- Track down a lost artifact
- Find evidence to clear a suspect or prove a culprit

SPACE-TIME BREACH
- Heroes interact with past or future selves
- Dinosaurs roam the earth
- Criminals with future tech robbing banks
- Time loop
- Wormholes moving people to faraway places

SUDDEN COLLAPSE
- Bridge falls out from under Heroes or Civilians
- Floors in an office building crumble underfoot
- Any suddenly unstable footing
- Avalanche
- Fissures form due to earthquake or superhero/villain activity
- House implodes due to supernatural forces

THE BRIDGE IS OUT
- Bridge slowly begins to collapse while Heroes or Civilians are on it
- The regular path is blocked, forcing Heroes through a more dangerous environment

TICKING CLOCK/BOMB
- An actual bomb that will explode when the timer hits zero
- Any event that would be catastrophic or detrimental, giving our Heroes a limited amount of time to do other things

TRAINING FOR A SPECIFIC FOE
- Research a specific foe's weakness
- Spar with mentor to improve abilities
- Internal reflection on previous encounters

WEATHER IS OUT OF CONTROL
- Reverse hurricane brings down frigid air from upper atmosphere, causing new ice age
- F5 Tornadoes
- Cult/terrorist group with a weather machine
- Solar storms
- Forest fires due to extreme drought

LOCATION, LOCATION, LOCATION

Every film has to take place somewhere. A good location scout can save time and money and elevate the entire project. Too bad this film didn't have one of those.

Now that the plot points have been established, it is time to specify a couple locations important to the film's narrative. The Active Player is expected - even encouraged - to create new locations as needed, but it helps to have an idea of where the Act One Inciting Incident and the Act Three Final Showdown will happen. These two locations are the bedrock of building the story; it's important to know where the story starts, and where it's destined to end.

The two locations to make now are:

- The Opening Scene
- The Final Stage

THE OPENING SCENE

The Opening Scene is where the story begins. There are no random tables for locations – locations should be tailored to fit the criteria already established for the scene. Once the players decide on a location, they should name and describe it. Start with a generic name – like Secret Headquarters, the Greasy Spoon Diner, or the Abandoned Mansion – and mold it to become more specific as the location takes shape. For example, the Abandoned Mansion might eventually become the Abandoned Wentworth Estate.

Finally, give the location a quirky detail called the Worst Possible Thing. This is one thing that could go wrong at this location that would add a lot of drama to any Heroes that happen to be there at the time. The Worst Possible Thing should be thematically appropriate to the genre of the story. It should be both fun and dramatic - just in case it becomes part of the game as a Minor Obstacle due to a Critical Failure.

Making new locations is part of the game. Anytime you need to do so, try to use the same format, giving the location a name and a brief description, at minimum. The Worst Possible Thing is only needed if it comes up, and can be decided in the moment.

Here are some examples of Opening Scene locations, with descriptions of how they might be utilized in the narrative:

THE OLD MANSION

A massive three-story house on a seaside cliff, rumored to have secret rooms and passages. It's been abandoned for years, but rumors of sounds and light have started circulating lately.

- Site of strange stories, dating back to the 1940s
- Local teens claim it's haunted

Worst Thing Possible: If the vengeful spirits awaken, they'll attack anyone inside, which might cause the mansion to catch fire or collapse into the sea.

THE ENGINE ROOM

The engine room of a ship or a train, or the room with the motors to run industrial pumps or elevators.

- Tight spaces, loose panels, exposed wires
- Very hot
- Hard to access

Worst Possible Thing: If the coolant fails, the engine will overheat and explode.

SHEB'S SALOON

Sheb's is a two-story taphouse, with a piano in the corner and rooms for rent upstairs. There are always a few drinkers and gamblers in the taproom, no matter the hour.

- Downstairs has a bar, a piano, and a stage for performances
- Upstairs has rooms with beds
- Long bar with wobbly stools and spittoons

Worst Possible Thing: If the old copper mines below town collapse, Sheb's could fall into the sinkhole.

THE UNDERGROUND CASINO

A secret casino, as extravagant as any on the Las Vegas Strip, catering to illicit gamblers of every size, shape, and nationality. Openly armed security guards patrol the floors.

- Only known to criminals with enough money to be clients
- Smoke filled rooms
- Guards looking for an excuse to use violence

Worst Possible Thing: Everyone is packing; if a gun fight breaks out, no one is safe.

THE COURTHOUSE

The Halls of Justice. An imposing building in the town square, whose size and stature hint at an oppressive element in town governance.

- A mixture of old stone and new wood constructions
- The judicial center of the regime
- The halls echo with the whispers of the condemned

Worst Possible Thing: If the restless spirits of the wrongly condemned manifest, they will seek retribution against those who convicted them – and anyone who gets in their way.

THE EXTRAVAGANT MALL

A large, sprawling complex of stores, selling all manner of consumer goods. The approaching holiday season has shoppers flocking in for gifts.

- Multiple floors of stores and kiosks, connected by a series of interior walkways
- Filled with thousands of holiday shoppers

Worst Possible Thing: If the mall is the target of an attack or natural disaster, thousands of shoppers stand in harm's way.

THE FINAL STAGE

Since the BBEG, the Plot, and the Obstacles have all been chosen, there is enough information to establish the Final Stage. Knowing where the story is going to end gives the players a basic roadmap to follow as they collectively build scenes during the earlier parts of the game.

Using the same process as the Opening Scene, create a Final Stage location appropriate to your story: the clocktower at high noon, an abandoned space station, or the villain's secret lair, hidden in a volcano.

Here are some examples of Final Stage locations, with descriptions of how they might be utilized in the narrative:

DALKHIOR'S LAIR

The villain's lair is built inside of an active volcano, with lava seeping down the walls and acting as partitions to subdivide rooms. The facility is filled with state-of-the-art computer equipment.

- It's always hot
- Natural caverns mixed with advanced tech

Worst Possible Thing: If the lava tubes fail, the whole place will fill with lava.

MERCURIAL LABS

A multi-story building containing high-tech research and development labs specializing in DNA modification.

- Contains offices on the upper floors
- Secret labs under high security in the sub-basement.
- Building under tight high-tech security (retina scanners, implanted access chips, etc.)

Worst Possible Thing: Some of the experiments are deadly. If something were to escape containment, it could threaten the world.

THE MOON

The large natural satellite orbiting the Earth, visible in the sky at night.

- Cold, desolate, and distant
- Difficult to get to
- No breathable atmosphere

Worst Possible Thing: If the Heroes make a mistake, the moon could fall out of orbit and crash into the Earth.

ATLANTIS REBORN

The ancient city has risen from the depths. The majestic buildings are slowly draining from eons of being submerged.

- City covered in kelp, barnacles, and coral
- Still oddly intact, despite being buried for millennia
- Eerily empty

Worst Possible Thing: If people start poking around, they might accidentally activate an ancient weapon.

CREATING SUPPORTING CHARACTERS

While the Heroes are the main characters, and the story will focus on them, they need some Supporting Characters to interact with. Who better to put into danger than a former lover, a favorite teacher, or a sibling? Who can the Heroes turn to when they need help but their former mentor, a grandparent who harbors a secret, or a retired super-spy?

Going around the table, each player creates a Supporting Character for the story. Each Supporting Character is created similarly to locations: give them a name, a brief description including physical details, and a personality.

Create a diverse cast of Supporting Characters that fit the genre and story. They can be created in a vacuum, with each player working on their own for a few minutes, or as a table activity. It's fun to have the players create and present these Supporting Characters to the table, but they're less likely to have overlapping features when created by the group.

The point of these Supporting Characters is to give the Heroes someone to connect with in the story: someone in danger who needs to be saved, or someone with information they might need. These Supporting Characters can be sympathetic figures, antagonistic rivals, or innocent bystanders who get put in harm's way.

EXAMPLE SUPPORTING CHARACTERS

TOMMY HOLLANDER-CRATCHIT
Computer genius kid from the slums. Really shy, easily scared, loves machines more than people, easy to impress.

VANESSA WATSON
Admin assistant to "The Wizard" (evil tech CEO). Highly intelligent, but oblivious to the truth about her boss.

SARAH PRUITT
Thirty-something Harvard grad. Currently working for the Innocence Project and running a soup kitchen. Driven to see social justice in and out of the courtroom.

LAFAYETI
A French-born Yeti living in rural Oklahoma.

ZOREN
A witty, sarcastic safe cracker. Best hands in the business, whose eyes are failing. They rely on their apprentice to help them get from job to job.

Since *Action 12 Cinema* is a roleplaying game, someone may need to roleplay a Supporting Character when they appear in a scene. Ideally, when an Active Player first introduces a Supporting Character, one of the other players takes control of them and plays them whenever they're in a scene for the remainder of the game.

As this is a GM-less game, it doesn't always need to be the same player. If something happens where one player has multiple characters in a scene - maybe their own Hero and a Supporting Character or two - they can ask another player to take over and roleplay that character for them.

As in all things, let "Is this fun?" be your guide. If it's fun for both the player and the table to watch this one-person performance of multiple characters interacting, that's great. Just keep it short - we want everyone to play as much as possible.

If a new Supporting Character needs to be created during the game, just jot down their details onto a notecard for everyone to see. It's okay to have a bunch of nameless/faceless extras in a crowded scene; not everyone at the local bar or hanging out on the beach needs to be a Supporting Character. But maybe, when the cybernetic shark attacks, a particular beach-goer will become important enough to earn a full description, making them a Supporting Character.

If the players are struggling with ideas for their supporting character, have someone look up the cast list of a favorite action movie on IMDB.com. It's a good way to shortcut the process.

BULLETPROOF FURNITURE

"How 'bout a few pieces of Granny's HARD CANDY?"

HOLDING OUT FOR A HERO

With all the ground work that's been laid, from knowing the BBEG and their dastardly scheme to where the story begins and ends and who some of the Supporting Characters are, it's now time to fill in the rest of the blanks and create some Heroes.

Good characters have a depth to them, a gravitas where what they don't say can be more important than what they do. A single look can express a wave of information and deep emotion. Our story doesn't have room for good characters. We get Action Movie Heroes, dammit, and we're damn glad to have them!

Player characters are broadly defined, with vague backstories and a penchant for saying exactly what they're feeling so it's obvious, even when it's already obvious - saying it just makes it doubly obvious.

Heroes in **Action 12 Cinema** have the following characteristics:

- Name
- Description
- Attributes
- Skills
- Relationships
- Heroic Traits
- Achilles' Heel
- Personal Crisis

NAME

What's in a name? Not much at all for some movies, but for others: everything. **Action 12 Cinema** is about the types of movies where the Hero's name is often on-the-nose shorthand for the character and the journey they're on. The name can be important to the Hero's character design, or an afterthought.

ACTION 12 CINEMA
- Character Sheet -

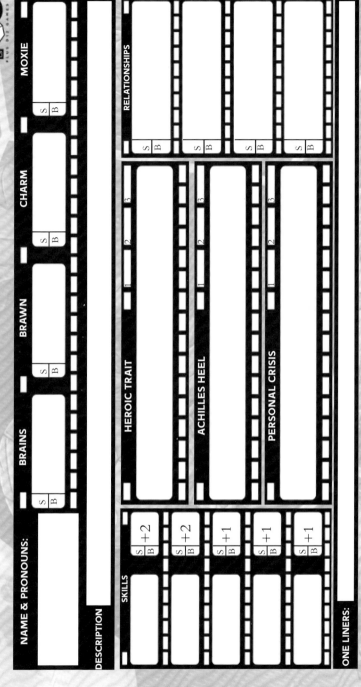

NAME & PRONOUNS:

DESCRIPTION

BRAINS S B

BRAWN S B

CHARM S B

MOXIE S B

SKILLS

S B +2

S B +2

S B +1

S B +1

S B +1

HEROIC TRAIT 1 2 3

ACHILLES HEEL 1 2 3

PERSONAL CRISIS 1 2 3

RELATIONSHIPS

S B

S B

S B

S B

ONE LINERS:

Some famous, and not-so-famous, Action Movie Hero names, for inspiration:

John Matrix	Marion 'Cobra'	Lara Croft
John Rambo	Cobretti	Leeloo
Dutch	Valentine McKee	Furiosa
Jericho Cane	Terry Leather	Hanna Heller
Mason Storm	James Bond	Sarah Connor
Gibson	Marshall Lawson	Ellen Ripley
Rickenbacker	John McClane	Shuri
John Spartan	Nico Toscani	Rey
Chance Boudreaux	Max Rockatanasky	Okoye
Snake Plissken	JJ McQuade	Switch
Lincoln Hawk	Matt Hunter	Tank
Johnny Rico	Joe Armstrong	John Wick
	Trinity	

DESCRIPTION

What does the character look like? What are some personality traits? This section is left vague on purpose, so each player can determine what descriptions they think are important. Some may want a lot of physical description, while others may have none at all, and instead fill this space with "A Man Out of Time," or "A Lonely Woman Looking for Love and Kicking Ass as She Does It."

Keep in mind, there's nothing that says the character can't be an anthropomorphized swarm of telepathic squirrels in a trench coat. If that sort of character fits in the story's genre, go for it!

ATTRIBUTES

In *Action 12 Cinema*, characters have four attributes.

Brains represent the Hero's intellect and problem solving skills. Characters who are scientists, hackers, or engineers likely have a high Brains score.

Brawn represents the Hero's physical strength. Characters who are barbarians, soldiers, or have been physically enhanced by a supernatural source likely have a high Brawn score.

Charm represents the Hero's social and emotional IQ: how well they navigate through social situations, as well as being able to encourage, inspire, lead, or even manipulate others. Diplomats, politicians, and military leaders likely have a high Charm score.

Moxie represents the Hero's force of determination or nerves. It also serves as this game's measure of luck or grit. Characters who get by on determination or sheer luck have a high Moxie score. When in doubt, Moxie is anything that isn't Brains, Brawn, or Charm.

BRAINS	BRAWN	CHARM	MOXIE
S B	S B	S B	S B

There is a space beneath each Attribute labeled on the Character Sheet, as pictured above. Each Attribute is assigned a score: one is a +2, two are each +1, and the remaining one is a 0. These numbers reflect how many d12s the Hero's Attributes add to the Dice Pool, if any.

The mechanics of **Action 12 Cinema** are pretty loose by design. It's almost always possible to roll using the Hero's best Attribute, but sometimes the narrative or mechanics of the game may force the player to roll with a suboptimal Dice Pool. Since failure in **Action 12 Cinema** just means more fun, it might be more interesting to roll with a lesser Attribute, just to see what happens. It can make for a pivotal story moment when the genius hacker character suddenly decides to throw hands at the alien cyborg bounty hunter.

Beyond the mechanics of building the Dice Pool, how Attributes are allocated will help flesh out and solidify the character.

SKILLS

There are five empty boxes on the Character Sheet for listing Skills. Two Skills are rated as +2, and three Skills as +1, which add 2 dice and 1 die to the Dice Pool, respectively. The Active Player can only leverage one Skill for each Dice Pool.

Each Hero should have at least two Skills defined before play begins. All five can be defined at the beginning, or the player can choose to wait and fill them in later, creating one of those action movie tropes where a Hero suddenly has a Skill they never hinted at, which gives them exactly the edge they need to survive/win the day.

But what is a Skill? Great question! Here's the answer: Skills are anything you want them to be. There is no standardized list of Skills to choose from; the player may create any Skill they wish.

When it comes time to build a Dice Pool, the player may use a Skill, if it applies to the action being taken. Since there is no GM to adjudicate, it's up to the Active Player's sensibilities - and the credulity of the other players - to agree if the Skill makes sense or not. Mechanically speaking, it makes the most sense to create some narratively broad Skills that can be easily applied to various situations, but it's also fun to create something super specific and try to build towards a situation where that super specific Skill makes sense.

EXAMPLES OF SKILLS

Acrobatics
Action Combat
Arcana
Blacksmithing
Bureaucracy
Code Breaking
Computers
Counterfeiting
Cryptid Mating Calls
Dance Fighting
Deception
Detection
Engineering
Fencing
Firearms
Firefighting

Forgery
Gambling
Gymnastics
Hacking
Herbalism
Hypnotism
I Can Drive Anything
I Can Fix Anything
I Skate Through Life
I Watch a Lot of Movies
I've Read a Lot of Books
Law
Lock Picking
Military Training

Monster Lore
Mountaineering
Obscure Knowledge
Parkour
Private Eye
Science
SCUBA Diving
Seduction
Sleight of hand
Spelunking
Streetwise
Technophile
Underworld Contacts
Weapons from Anything
Wrestling

RELATIONSHIPS

It's been said that, "It's not what you know, but who you know." In **Action 12 Cinema**, it's both. Each Hero should begin the game with at least one defined Relationship between their Hero and another Hero or one of the Supporting Characters. The Relationship can be between any Hero or Supporting Character, not just the ones that the player created. The Active Player may choose to Leverage a Relationship to add a d12 to their Dice Pool. Much like Skills, Relationships can be broadly or specifically defined.

A Relationship can be Leveraged in a couple ways. For example, if that character is physically in the same scene as the Active Player's Hero and the fiction supports them helping, the Active Player can Leverage the Relationship, compelling them to assist. They could also provide emotional support or inspiration, because You Can't Let Your Daughter Down Again. Not this time!

There are four open spaces on the Character Sheet for Relationships. It is recommended that you begin play with at least one established Relationship (but two would be better). A Hero can start with all four, and players will have opportunities to change Relationships, or add new ones, during the game. But hey, that's why pencils have erasers, right?

When creating a Relationship with another player's Hero, it is important to make sure they're on board with that Relationship, especially if it's familial or romantic. It isn't necessary to get another player's permission to create a Relationship with a Supporting Character they created, as long as the Relationship doesn't conflict with the established fiction, but if two different Heroes want to say the same Supporting Character is their sibling, then everyone needs to be on board with that. Communication and consent are critical when creating these Relationships.

EXAMPLES OF RELATIONSHIPS

When I left the military *[HERO NAME]* helped me adjust to civilian life.

I had to break a rule to help a friend. *[HERO NAME]* covered for me and I'm not sure why.

[HERO NAME] is my best friend. They'd never let me down. I can't fail them.

[SUPPORTING CHARACTER] is my child who doesn't know what I do and I want to keep that from them.

[SUPPORTING CHARACTER] looks up to me like I'm a Hero from a story. I won't let them see me otherwise.

[HERO NAME] and I served in the same military unit.

[SUPPORTING CHARACTER] Is a student of mine. I see their potential even though they don't see it in themselves.

[SUPPORTING CHARACTER] and I connected on a speed date. I thought it went great but they never called me back.

[HERO NAME] is my partner. I have their back and they've always got mine.

HEROIC TRAIT

Ordinarily, Heroes aren't ordinary - they're Heroes. What makes this Hero so special? In most B-grade action movies, there's usually a single defining quality that makes the Hero a Hero and not a Supporting Character.

During the game, the player can Leverage their Heroic Trait up to three times to re-roll a Dice Pool and try to get a better result. They may use their Heroic Trait once to reroll any dice in their Dice Pool that aren't 1s, or use it twice to reroll anything, including 1s. When they decide to use their Heroic Trait in this way, they can decide if the narration reflects a nearly failed attempt that ultimately succeeds, or if the audience only sees the second, hopefully more successful, attempt.

EXAMPLES OF HEROIC TRAITS

A Born Leader	Honest	Protective
Always Prepared	Inspirational	Resilient
Brave	Intelligent	Selfless
Caring	Just	Stoic
Determined	Kind	Too Dumb to Fail
Eternally Optimistic	Master Tactician	Wise

ONE AT A TIME

CAMERA PANNING AROUND CIRCLE

ACHILLES' HEEL

Well, nobody is perfect, right? Not even broadly defined characters with shallow motivations and on-the-nose names. Everyone has something that holds them back, or has a chance to make a bad situation worse. For some, it's not knowing when to quit, or always assuming they're the smartest person in the room. Maybe they forget their own strength sometimes. Whatever it is, it's often useful, but could bite them in the ass.

The player may leverage their Hero's Achilles' Heel up to three times per game, which allows them to add two d12s to their Dice Pool. This is the only way to exceed the normal Dice Pool size limit of five dice. Any 1s rolled when using a Hero's Achilles' Heel cannot be rerolled by invoking their Heroic Trait, and they count as two Setbacks instead of one, meaning they are more likely to trigger a Critical Failure. This is a very high risk, high reward type of decision.

EXAMPLES OF ACHILLES' HEELS
Arrogant
Collateral Damage is Fine as long as I succeed.
Failure isn't an option.
Honest to a Fault
I can always talk my way out of a situation
I don't need skill, I have luck.
Inappropriate humor
I work best under pressure
Never surrender.
Overconfident
Reckless

PERSONAL CRISIS

A staple of bad (but fun!) Action Movie Heroes is that while they are, without a doubt, the right person to be an action hero, their personal life is a mess. They're about to lose their job, their house, their spouse, or all three. Their parents don't understand them. They're battling some sort of an addiction. Their kid hates them, or they're not ready to have kids, and it's straining the relationship.

The good news is that, during the course of the movie, they often get a chance to examine their life and maybe - just maybe - solve their own problems, while also solving the world's.

There is no mechanical benefit to solving the Hero's Personal Crisis; it's purely a tool to drive their personal narrative. The Active Player may choose to invoke their Hero's Personal Crisis on their turn, removing one d12 from their Dice Pool. If the roll using the reduced Dice Pool yields progress towards an active Obstacle, the Active Player may then also check off one tick on their Hero's Personal Crisis track. If a player is able to check all three Personal Crisis boxes for their Hero, they will be able to resolve their Hero's Personal Crisis in the game's final scene.

The Personal Crisis is a prompt to help a player roleplay their Hero and guide their narrative decisions, as well as build or change Relationships during the game. It is optional, and some players may not interact with it at all. It's only as important as the player wants it to be. Ideally, a player will mark off one tick in each Act, but there is no hard rule that it must be done once per Act.

EXAMPLES OF PERSONAL CRISES

I ended a relationship because of how others viewed it, and now I regret it.

I think my former lover is the one that got away. How can I win them back?

My fear of failure has caused me to become paralyzed with indecision.

Can I learn to love again after what happened last time?

I made a mistake and someone got hurt. Can I learn to live with it and move on?

I let someone else take the blame for something I did. How can I make it right?

My job has always come first. Maybe it's time to change that?

Not that the war is over, who am I?

My stepson doesn't love me.

I've been a coward all my life. Can I be the Hero when called upon?

ACTION MOVIE HERO ONE-LINERS

We all know them, we all love them: iconic lines delivered by the Action Movie Heroes, just before or just after dispatching one of the villains or their minions. What Action Movie game would be complete without at least a nod to this iconic part of the action movie genre? Not this one.

If a player is able to drop a perfect one-liner during the game, then all Heroes can take a free Healing. Perfect is, of course, relative; did the table love it? If so, then it's perfect.

There is a space on the Character Sheet for the player to write down their One-Liners, so they can circle back to them later. Players aren't expected to create them ahead of time, but they're free to do so. It may even end up as the Hero's Catchphrase!

TROPES

Tropes are a part of life when it comes to action movies, especially the bad (but fun!) ones. A trope is nothing more than a commonplace, recognizable plot element, theme, or visual cue implicit in the action movie genre.

Use the charts below to generate a list of five Tropes for Act One. Each Trope requires two rolls of a d12; the first roll determines the table to be used, and the second roll determines the result on that table. Each result will give an option of two Tropes, and the table chooses which they prefer.

Write them down on the Production Sheet in the Act One Tropes spaces. During the game, any Active Player may Leverage one of these Tropes and bring it into the scene narration to get another d12 for their Dice Pool. A Trope can't increase the Active Player's Dice Pool to more than five dice, but it's a great way to increase the size of the Dice Pool when the player is unable to use their best Attributes or Skills. A Trope can be used multiple times per Act, but it can only be Leveraged once.

At the end of each Act, any unused Tropes are moved to the new Act, and any Tropes which have been Leveraged are replaced from the tables. If a Trope isn't used and the players aren't sure they want to keep it, they're free to ditch it and create a whole new list of five for each Act. If there are specific Tropes that players wish to use, they can use them instead of rolling for a random Trope.

A full list of these Tropes, with descriptions, can be found starting on page 87.

CAMERA MOVES BACKWARD AS BLIMP DIMINISHES IN BACKGROUND

TROPES TABLE 1

D12	OPTIONS		
1	Colossus Climb	or	Kitchen Chase
2	Unlimited Ammo	or	This Way to Certain Death
3	Universal Driver's License	or	Walk the Plank
4	Cavalry Betrayal	or	Mission Briefing
5	No Collateral Damage	or	Rope Bridge
6	Cave Mouth	or	Bullet Catch
7	Forced to Fight	or	Clifftop Caterwauling
8	Absurdly Sharp Blade	or	Kissus Interruptus
9	One at a Time	or	Death Course
10	Rising Water, Rising Tension	or	Stab the Scorpion
11	Walking Away from an Explosion	or	Forging Scene
12	Superhero Landing	or	All I Have Left is This!

TROPES TABLE 2

D12	OPTIONS		
1	Vapor Trail	or	Not Dead Yet!
2	Skeleton Key Card	or	And Mission Control Rejoiced
3	Trick-and-Follow Ploy	or	Marked Bullet
4	Troll Bridge	or	Pit Trap
5	Train-top Battle	or	Life-or-Limb Decision
6	Imminent Danger Clue	or	Concert Climax
7	Indy Escape	or	Hollywood CB
8	Giving the Sword to the Noob	or	Sheep in Wolf's Clothing
9	Powder Trail	or	Fast Roping
10	Kinda Busy Here	or	Banging for Help!
11	Instant Knots	or	Bathroom Break-Out
12	Supernatural Martial Arts	or	Delivery Guy Infiltration

TROPES TABLE 3

D12	OPTIONS		
1	Hey, Wait!	or	The Radio Dies First
2	Dead Man's Trigger Finger	or	Air Vent Passageway
3	Weaponized Car	or	Caught in a Snare
4	Backing into Danger	or	Nitro Express
5	Deadly Gas	or	Gunpoint Banter
6	Stealth Hi/Bye	or	No OSHA Compliance
7	Improvised Parachute	or	"Open!" Says Me
8	Human Chess	or	Desperate Object Catch
9	Trojan Horse	or	Non-Fatal Explosions
10	Ceiling Smash	or	Catch a Falling Star
11	Futile Hand Reach	or	Shark Pool
12	Sky Heist	or	My Name is Inigo Montoya

TROPES TABLE 4

D12	OPTIONS		
1	Emergency Stash	or	Diner Brawl
2	Juggle-Fu	or	Bulletproof Human Shield
3	Body Bag Trick	or	Dish Dash
4	Impressive Pyrotechnics	or	Bad Habits
5	Enemy Rising Behind	or	Exotic Weapon Supremacy
6	Government Agency of Fiction	or	That's Bait
7	Impossible Mission Collapse	or	Dog Pile of Doom
8	Unfeasible Vehicle	or	Don't You Give Up On Me!
9	Chekhov's Exhibit	or	Hands off My Fluffy!
10	Ejection Seat	or	Mexican Standoff
11	Water Wake-Up	or	The Anticipator
12	Hero Stole My Bike	or	Punched Across the Room

TROPES TABLE 5

D12	OPTIONS		
1	Cable-Car Action Sequence	or	Acoustic License
2	Exploding Fish Tanks	or	Morse Code
3	Smoke Out	or	Xantos Gambit
4	Cyanide Pill	or	Exposition Diagram
5	Gladiator Games	or	Paper-Thin Disguise
6	Clipboard of Authority	or	Enhance!
7	Road Sign Reversal	or	Car Cushion
8	You're the Bait	or	Badass Driver
9	Empty Quiver	or	Barrier-Busting Blow
10	"Unflinching Faith in the Brakes"	or	Cut the Red Wire, No. Wait! The Blue One
11	Death Trap	or	Vertical Kidnapping
12	Cobweb Jungle	or	Indy Hat Roll

TROPES TABLE 6

D12	OPTIONS		
1	Underside Ride	or	An Ass-Kicking Christmas
2	Hallway Fight	or	Prisoners with Jobs are Loose
3	Boomerang Comeback	or	Dead Foot Leadfoot
4	Shoot the Rope	or	Climb, Slip, Hang, Climb
5	Out-of-Character Alert	or	Trojan Prisoner
6	""He's Right Behind Me, Isn't He?""	or	The Big Inspirational Speech
7	And They Said [Blank] was a Waste of Time	or	Grave Robbing
8	Precarious Ledge	or	Shooting Something so it Blows Up!
9	Ceiling Cling	or	Dungeon Bypass
10	Giant Foot of Stomping	or	Bodyguard Babes
11	High Speed Chase	or	Conveniently Timed Guard
12	Ominous Walk	or	Tuck and Cover

TROPES TABLE 7

D12	OPTIONS		
1	Cacophony Cover Up	or	Durable Deathtrap
2	Punch! Punch! Punch! Uh, Oh!	or	Outside Ride
3	Bar Slide	or	"Hey, You!" Haymaker
4	Man on Fire	or	Hey, Catch!
5	Honor Among Thieves	or	Skeleton Key
6	Involuntary Group Split	or	The Precious, Precious Car
7	Hollywood Fire	or	Diving into the Truck
8	Hastily Made Prop	or	I Need No Ladders
9	Feed the Good Beastie	or	Bloodless Carnage
10	Not in This for Your Revolution	or	Take up My Sword
11	Reed Snorkel	or	Dirt Forcefield
12	Tactical Overlay	or	Action Dad

TROPES TABLE 8

D12	OPTIONS		
1	Emergency Cargo Dump	or	Unwilling Suspension
2	Slipped the Ropes	or	The Cavalry Arrives Late
3	The Idol's Blessing	or	We Don't Have the Budget for That
4	Almost Out of Oxygen	or	Those Were Only Their Scouts
5	Shoot the Fuel Tank	or	Bluff the Impostor
6	Flamethrower Backfire	or	Villain's Throne
7	Dressing as the Enemy	or	Adrenaline Makeover
8	Break out the Museum Piece	or	Action Girl
9	Wrong Wire	or	Instrument of Murder
10	Your Shoe is Untied	or	Quicksand Sucks!
11	Saw it in a Movie Once	or	Improvised Zipline
12	"Luck-based Search Technique"	or	Train Escape

TROPES TABLE 9

D12	OPTIONS		
1	Rooftop Confrontation	or	Plummet Perspective
2	Climbing the Cliffs of Insanity	or	Kidnapped from Behind
3	Action Insurance Gag	or	Disney Death
4	Inevitable Waterfall	or	Dead Man's Switch
5	Breaking the Bonds	or	Secret Underground Passage
6	Bombproof Appliance	or	Get the Gun Already!
7	Always a Bigger Fish	or	Let's Fight like Gentlemen
8	Hollywood Acid	or	Mirror Scare
9	Removing the Earpiece	or	Hardcore Parkour
10	Silent Running Mode	or	Bottled Heroic Resolve
11	Convenient Escape Boat	or	Acquired Poison Immunity
12	Implausible Fencing Powers	or	Hassle-Free Hotwire

TROPES TABLE 10

D12	OPTIONS		
1	"Hunting the Most Dangerous Game"	or	Big Heroic Run
2	Check the Visor	or	Contract on the Hitman
3	Action Dress Rip	or	Bookcase Passage
4	Dye or Die	or	"Locking MacGyver in the Store Cupboard"
5	Katanas are Just Better	or	Line in the Sand
6	Feed the Bad Beastie	or	Midair Repair
7	Harmless Freezing	or	Latex Perfection
8	Paying for the Action Scene	or	Cigar-Fuse Lighting
9	Ferris Wheel of Doom	or	Ceiling Crash
10	Bad-Guy Bar	or	Clockwork Prediction
11	Well, that's a Cliffhanger	or	Bulletproof Furniture
12	*Drool* Hello	or	1-Dimensional Thinking

TROPES TABLE 11

D12	OPTIONS		
1	Now It's My Turn!	or	Gasoline Dowsing
2	After-Action Healing Drama	or	Beast in the Maze
3	Bound and Gagged	or	Passing the Torch
4	Conveniently Timed Attack from Behind	or	Super Window Jump
5	Time Bomb	or	Facing the Bullets One-Liner
6	Soft Glass	or	Pin-Pulling Teeth
7	Goggles Do Something Unusual	or	The Scrounger
8	Great Escape	or	Percussive Prevention
9	Carnival of Killers	or	Improbable Cover
10	"If You're So Evil, Eat this Kitten!"	or	Action Mom
11	Deep Cover Agent	or	Cool and Unusual Punishment
12	Sword and Gun	or	Convenient Enemy Base

TROPES TABLE 12

D12	OPTIONS		
1	Wait, What's This?	or	Just a Kid
2	Foe-Tossing Charge	or	Danger with a Deadline
3	Out of Sight, Out of Mind	or	Flynning
4	10-Minute Retirement	or	Darkened Building Shootout
5	Decoy Hiding Place	or	Scary Surprise Party
6	Fighter-Launching Sequence	or	Outrun the Fireball
7	Unstoppable Rage	or	Flaming Emblem
8	Monumental Damage	or	Empty Elevator
9	Hitchhiking Heroes	or	"Action Film, Quiet Drama Scene"
10	Tired of Running	or	Keep Away
11	"Conveniently Placed Sharp Thing"	or	No One Will Follow This
12	Nerf Arm	or	Disaster-Dodging Doggo

Once Tropes have been selected, the Pre-Production Phase is complete, and the Production Phase can begin. Make sure everyone has all the info they need on their copy of the Production Sheet.

This break between Pre-Production and Production Phases is a great time to take a short break. Use the restroom, stretch your legs, and get a snack or a drink, then the Production Phase can begin!

THE PRODUCTION PHASE

The Production Phase of the game consists of the following sections:

- The Opening Credits Scenes
- Act One: The Inciting Incident
- Interstitial Scene (as needed/wanted)
- Act Two: The Rising Tension
- Interstitial Scene (as needed/wanted)
- Act Three: The Final Showdown
- Concluding Scenes
- Name the Movie
- Post-Credits Stinger (optional)
- Post-Game Discussion/Wrap-Up

This is a roadmap of how the game is designed to go, but each game is its own unique thing. It's okay if the game doesn't follow this path exactly.

THE OPENING CREDITS

Going around the table, each player gets an opportunity to introduce their character through an Opening Credits scene. These scenes are generally short, and don't involve roleplaying — at least, not between the Heroes. These are the scenes that give the audience their initial glimpse of the Heroes.

Sometimes these will be action scenes, showing the Heroes being their most badass selves in a previous crisis — the Superhero taking out several villains in quick succession, or the Martial Arts students taking their first steps toward becoming a Master. Other times, these may be quiet, even reflective, moments. Perhaps the Hero wakes up and goes about their normal domestic routine: coffee, a morning run, a shower, and breakfast.

These scenes should tell the audience something about the character. Do they live alone? Maybe they're recently divorced, and the bills are piling up. They look longingly at a neighbor, but they're too awkward to approach.

Each player should feel free to luxuriate in these opening scenes, to let the audience see their Heroes exactly as they want them to.

Since the Opening Scene and Inciting Incident have already been determined, the Opening Credits is a good way to place the Heroes in that scene. Each player should end their introduction in a way that connects to the Opening Scene. Perhaps the audience sees an alert at Headquarters warning of an impending disaster, a group text asking if the Heroes are en route to the birthday party, or scrolling cable news headlines that the Hero doesn't notice.

Once everyone has had a chance to set up their Hero through their Opening Credits scene, it's time to move on and open Act One.

ACT ONE: THE INCITING INCIDENT

At this point, one of the players becomes the first Active Player. This is usually the person who's been acting as Facilitator, but anyone can be the first Active Player if the table agrees. This first Active Player has some important work to do, as they finally get to put the specifics of the world into place and introduce the first Obstacle, as well as building and resolving the first Dice Pool.

Each player takes a turn as the Active Player, trying to address the current Obstacle, however it's been defined in your story. If the inciting incident is a Fight!, and the genre is a Creature Feature, this might be monstrous amphibians emerging from the water and attacking civilians. The Heroes may already be all together and being

KITCHEN CHASE

CAMERA STATIONARY AS RICH/CROW HORDE DASH PAST

attacked themselves, or they may be nearby to an attack so they can respond, and this first Obstacle is what brings them together. It may be easier to just say all the Heroes know each other and are together at the start of Act One, but the extra narrative challenge of having them start separately and build together can be a fun exercise and additional challenge for experienced players.

After a player takes their turn as the Active Player, they should not go again until every other player has had a turn. There are no hard rules for determining turn order. Going around the table, passing to the Hero that makes the most narrative sense, or passing to the next player with an idea are all equally viable.

It can be helpful to have some sort of token or card that can be flipped from a Ready for Action side to an I've Had My Turn side to help keep everyone on the same page. It's also okay for the same player to go last in one round and then first in the next round, if it makes sense narratively and the players are all okay with it.

The Active Player has nearly unlimited narrative control to describe what is happening. They can move in and out of scenes, through time and distance as they want, but should try to keep in mind that this is a movie. Using film language can help, saying things like:

EXAMPLE

"We open on a drone shot high above the ground. It swoops down for a close-up on a small fissure - a fault line is opening up and racing in a zigzag pattern. We can see a large city off in the distance.

We then do a hard cut to my Hero, in line at the DMV..."

At this point, the Active Player may want to do a short roleplay scene with their character waiting in line, and another player might be the overworked and uncaring DMV worker, or maybe their own Hero is also in line.

It's totally fine for other players to throw out ideas, offer suggestions, and even place their own Hero in a scene, but the Active Player still has control. At some point, they will decide it's time to roll their dice. This usually happens when they are confronting the Obstacle (they're attacking the cyber-robots from Mars), or when the Obstacle threatens them (they have to get to safety from a rushing tidal wave).

One of the keys of **Action 12 Cinema** is learning when to roll the Dice Pool. There are no hard and fast rules, but the roll should usually be made just before a dramatic moment. The Active Player then uses the Dice Pool results to guide the conclusion of their turn before passing control to the next player. In most cases, the first 85% of their turn is storytelling/roleplaying, then they roll the dice and use the results as a guide to finish the last 15%.

The results of the Dice Pool will either be:

- Critical Failure: They've made things worse.
- Activate a Villain Cutscene: No progress made.
- Incremental Success: Some progress was made.
- Complete Success: They've overcome the Obstacle.

Each time a player rolls their Dice Pool, they record their total net result. In Act One, it takes a cumulative total of 12 Successes to end the Act and move on to the Response/Reset scenes. Generally, it will take between 3 and 5 Active Player turns to overcome the Act One Obstacle.

RESPONSE/RESET SCENES

As a game focused on action - after all, it's in the title - the transition scenes that help advance a movie plot are present, but often an afterthought. After an Act ends, each player has the option to do one or more short non-rolling scenes, if they wish. These are similar to Opening Credits scenes, and allow for the Heroes to move locations, meet new people, get medical care, and do whatever they need to do before the next Obstacle is introduced. This is a good space for players to stretch their roleplaying muscles, but, ideally these scenes are brief. Players may also add or change a Relationship during this time, if it makes sense in the established fiction.

Players should use the Tropes charts and generate new Tropes for Act Two. Unused Tropes from Act One can be replaced or moved over into Act Two - whichever the players prefer.

ACT TWO: THE RISING TENSION

In Act Two, things are getting worse. The explosions are bigger, the stakes are higher, and all hope seems lost.

The players will be dealing with two overlapping Obstacles in this Act. Based on which Obstacles were assigned to Act Two during the Pre-Production Phase, the first Active Player in Act Two may decide to introduce them at the same time, or have one Obstacle for a few turns, then introduce the second before the first is fully resolved.

The idea is that the Heroes will need to split their actions between the two Obstacles, either with some Heroes dealing with one Obstacle while the others are dealing with the second one, or choosing each turn which Obstacles to engage with based on the narrative.

It takes 12 Successes to resolve each Obstacle in Act Two. Successes can only be assigned towards one Obstacle at a time. The exception to this rule is when a roll generates more Successes than required to resolve an Obstacle. In this case, any remaining Successes may be applied to the remaining Obstacle.

For example, if the Active Player gets five Successes, they can't apply three of them to one Obstacle and two to the other. But, if the first Obstacle only needs three more Successes to be resolved, they could apply the first three to the first Obstacle, reaching Complete Success, and then apply the two remaining Successes to the remaining Obstacle.

Once both Obstacles have been resolved, do another round of Response/Reset Scenes, then move into Act Three.

ACT THREE: THE FINAL SHOWDOWN

The Final Showdown may have been decided back during the Pre-Production Phase, but now it's time to see how the story changes between the outline and the performance.

Act Three is the story's grand finale, with the Heroes having to overcome three overlapping Obstacles. Two of the Obstacles are Minor Obstacles, which each have a value of 6 points, and the third is the Final Obstacle, which has a value of 12 points. Both of the Minor Obstacles must be resolved before Successes can be assigned towards resolving the Final Obstacle.

For example, if the three Obstacles in Act Three are Fight!, Magical Defenses, and Fight! (Fight! comes up a lot so it's okay to have it more than once), the first Minor Obstacle might be to Fight! against a horde of undead zombie minions. The second Minor Obstacle, Magical Defenses, might be a barrier which must be de-magicked or broken down by force - maybe a bit of both. Once both have been dealt with, then the Heroes can go toe-to-toe with the ancient necro-dragon-mancer...from Venus!

After resolving the Final Obstacle, the Heroes finally emerge victorious. This resolution is called the Final Success, and indicates the end of the mechanical portion of the game. Each player gets to

ALWAYS A BIGGER FISH

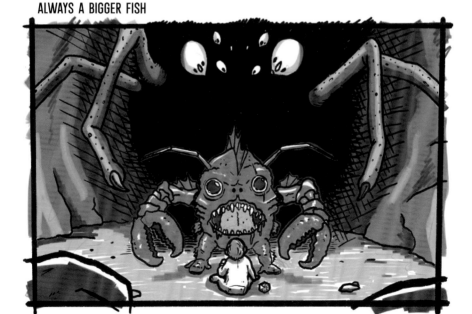

narrate one scene, to show the audience how the experience of the movie changed their Hero; where their Hero gets to reunite with their loved ones, reorient themselves to a new world, or finally take a moment to close their eyes and feel the sunrise on their face. If a player was able to complete their Personal Crisis track, this scene is the time to show that change in action.

POST-CREDIT STINGER

This is an optional scene, but if anyone wants to give a post-credits stinger setting up the inevitable, lower-budget, direct-to-video/streaming sequel movie, now's the time.

NAME THE MOVIE

Now that this Action Movie experience is complete, ask the players if anyone has a good title for this cinematic masterpiece. As previously stated, "good" is relative; many action movies, like their Heroes, have overly melodramatic or on-the-nose names.

WRAP-UP!

Congratulations, you've made your movie! Hopefully everyone had a great time. Set a few minutes aside for a wrap-up discussion. Go over your favorite rolls, scenes, and One-Liners. Discuss what changes, if any, you'd like to make for next time.

THE MECHANICS OF THE GAME

Now that the overview of **Action 12 Cinema** is complete, it's time to take a deeper dive into the game's dice rolling mechanics. This section will cover how to build a Dice Pool, and how to interpret and alter the results of Dice Pool rolls.

BUILDING A DICE POOL

When the Active Player is taking their turn, trying to address the current Obstacle(s), they begin by narrating and roleplaying the scene however they like. At some point they'll stop, state their intent, and then roll some dice. Based on the results of the roll, they will finish their turn by narrating and roleplaying how those results reinforce or change the fiction, and then pass to the next Active Player.

The Dice Pool always starts with one d12. While an ideal Dice Pool will have four or five dice, the Active Player will always roll at least one d12. When rolling fewer than four dice, consider trying to bring in a Trope, leverage a Relationship, or create a new Skill. It's fine to roll fewer than four dice on occasion, but consistently rolling three or fewer dice will lengthen the game.

To build the Dice Pool, choose which of the Hero's Attributes best connects to the action the Hero is performing, and add that Attribute's value to the Dice Pool. Keep in mind that there is no GM deciding which Attribute to use for any given roll. So long as the Active Player can rationalize the use of an Attribute in such a way as to get the table to agree, they can use whichever Attribute they choose.

Next, determine if the Hero has any Skills that are useful for the action being rolled. If so, add a number of dice equal to that Skill's value to the Dice Pool. If not, and the Hero still has unassigned Skills, the Active Player may create an appropriate Skill for the action, and add the new Skill's value to the Dice Pool. Only one Skill can be leveraged per Dice Pool.

If the Active Player's Hero has a Relationship with another character, they may choose to Leverage that Relationship to gain one more d12. The other character might be in the scene with them, or be in contact from another location. As long as the Active Player can rationalize how the Relationship is assisting their Hero in the scene, it can be Leveraged for an extra die.

Ideally, an Active Player's Dice Pool should have five d12s. If the Dice Pool has fewer than five dice in it, the Active Player may invoke a Trope to add one more d12 to the Dice Pool. The Dice Pool can have a maximum of five d12s, or seven d12s if the Active Player chooses to Leverage their Hero's Achilles' Heel.

Let's look at an example.

<hr>

EXAMPLE

Michael's Hero, Ray 'Ray Gun' Gunnerson, has found himself inexplicably teleported from his home on Earth to another planet on the far side of the galaxy, and is being accosted by a 3-eyed Tri-clops. So far, he has managed to keep away from the grasping brute while he tries to figure out what has happened and where he is (This first Obstacle would be a Fight!). Michael decides it's time to roll his first Dice Pool.

Michael begins with the default one die in his Dice Pool. He has been describing Ray athletically dodging away from the Tri-clops, so Brawn makes the most sense for which Attribute to use. Ray's Brawn is his best attribute, rated at +2.

Michael adds those two d12s to his Dice Pool, which is now at three. The actions Ray is taking match pretty well to the Crossfit exercise he does as a professional football player, so he creates a new +1 Skill - Crossfit - and Leverages that to increase his Dice Pool to four dice. Michael wants to roll a full Dice Pool of five dice, so he decides to Leverage his Relationship with his girlfriend Wren Carden. Wren was with him when that science experiment went awry and teleported him here - wherever that is - and she might also be in danger nearby. Ray needs to get away from the Tri-clops if he has any hope in finding her.

1 d12 + **2** *(Brawn Attribute)* + **1** *(Crossfit Skill)* + **1** *(Relationship with Wren)*
= **5** *d12s for his Dice Pool*

CHECK THE VALUES

Once the Dice Pool has been built, the Active Player rolls all of the dice and checks the results. The values have the following results:

D12	RESULT
1	Setback
2-7	Blank
8-11	Success
12	Heroic Success

Each resulting 1 creates one Setback. Each 12 rolled creates a Heroic Success, which counts as two Successes and grants the Active Player an additional bonus, which is detailed later.

CALCULATE THE NET RESULT

Compare the number of Setbacks to the number of Successes. If there are more Successes than Setbacks, subtract the Setbacks from the Successes and apply the result as progress towards resolving an Obstacle. If there are more Setbacks than Successes, the result is a Critical Failure, and if there are an equal number of Setbacks and Successes, no progress is made and a Villain Cutscene is triggered.

INCREMENTAL SUCCESS

Obstacles come into play with a value of 12, and Minor Obstacles with a value of 6. Outside of some wildly improbable dice rolls, this means that resolving an Obstacle will require more than one player taking a turn as the Active Player. If a Dice Pool roll is successful, subtract the number of net Successes from the current value of the Obstacle.

If the new value of the Obstacle isn't 0 or less, the action and dice roll resulted in an Incremental Success. This means that progress has been made, and the fiction of the world can reflect this new (better than before) situation, but the Obstacle hasn't been fully resolved. The Active Player's narration of the results as they end their turn should reflect this fact.

Any big action set piece from your favorite action movie can be broken down to mirror how Obstacles work in this game. For example, if the Obstacle is Find the Missing Person, the Active Player might narrate now they're reaching out to their underworld contacts to try and get a lead. They build their Dice Pool, using their Charm Attribute, the Private Investigator Skill, and Leveraging their Relationship with a Supporting Character who is a known criminal. They get some successes, but not enough to reduce the Obstacles value to 0 or less, so this is an Incremental Success.

Perhaps the informant saw them recently at a seedy dive bar, spawning a new Location, or maybe they tell the Hero where they are NOT: that the person hasn't been seen at any of their regular hangouts for a week or so. The Active Player could end their turn narrating/roleplaying their interaction with their contact. The party learns something that narrows down the search, but the search continues and play passes to another player.

On occasion, the fiction of a scene may play out in a way that the Hero of the Active Player is taking a backseat. Perhaps a high Charm Hero is commanding a bumbling sheriff to, "Shoot the monster!" The sheriff is firing a gun, but the Active Player still builds and rolls a Dice Pool - in this case, using their Charm and maybe a manipulation Skill to convince the sheriff to shoot at the monster.

COMPLETE SUCCESS

Eventually an Active Player will roll enough Successes to reduce the current Obstacle's value to 0 or less. At that point the Obstacle is resolved, and the Active Player's narration includes the change in the fiction to account for that Complete Success. They found the person, put out the fire, and stopped the ship from sinking. They diffused the bomb, turned off the weather machine, and flew away from the prison in a plume of snow. They've done it!

If that is the last Obstacle for the current Act, the Complete Success ends the Act and play moves to the next scene, where each player gets a chance to narrate/roleplay a scene without any rolls, clarifying their response to what has happened so far and refocusing them for the next part of the story.

The last Complete Success in the game - the resolution of the Final Obstacle in Act Three - is called the Final Success. This indicates the end of the mechanical portion of the game; there are no further Dice Pools to be formed, no more Heroic High Fives to give out. Once the Final Success has been achieved, the game moves into the Concluding Scenes, and becomes purely narrative.

CRITICAL FAILURE

A Critical Failure is triggered when a Dice Pool roll results in more Setbacks than Successes. This means things get worse, not better.

A Critical Failure adds four points to the value of the current Obstacle that was being rolled against, up to its original value. So, if the current Obstacle has had five Success applied to it, reducing its current value to seven, a Critical Failure would increase the Obstacle's value to eleven. The Active Player narrates the way the Critical Failure affects the Heroes and complicates the scene.

An Obstacle's value can never be higher than its starting value. If adding four points back to an Obstacle would take it above its starting value, add a new Minor Obstacle instead. This new Obstacle can be randomly generated by referring to the charts beginning on page 32, or the Active Player may choose or create one that makes narrative sense based on what is already occurring. This might be a great time to consider the Worst Possible Thing for the current location, if one was made.

With each Critical Failure, the Active Player should end their turn by narrating/roleplaying this new situation. Describe how the Hero's actions failed or did not work as intended, and how things have gotten worse. Remain true to the established fiction. If they were trying to break into a building, maybe security was alerted. If they're fighting Ghost Pirates, maybe their ship has started to sink. It doesn't matter narratively if their action directly caused the new situation or not, as long as the situation has been escalated as determined by the Critical Failure at the end of their turn.

ACTIVATE A VILLAIN CUTSCENE, A.K.A. NOTHING NEVER HAPPENS

When the result of a Dice Pool roll has zero net Successes, it is considered neither a success nor a failure. This might happen if the number of Successes equal the number of Setbacks, or if all of the dice come up as Blanks. While this may happen only rarely, it's not very exciting.

So, instead of the Active Player narrating/roleplaying nothing changing, they instead get to do a short cutscene where the audience sees what the BBEG and their forces are up to. Maybe they're working against the Heroes' actions directly (which is why, in the fiction, their efforts were neutralized), or maybe the audience is just getting a better glimpse at what their devious plan is.

The villain cutscenes don't change anything mechanically, but they do establish fiction which should be followed as the story advances.

STRESS AND BREAKING

There are no hit points or damage indicators for characters in *Action 12 Cinema*. That's because they're Action Movie Heroes, and they never die unless the script calls for it - and even then, only at the most dramatically appropriate time. What does happen is their lives get harder.

Any time a 1 is rolled in a Dice Pool, one of the elements used to build that Dice Pool takes Stress. Each Attribute, Skill, and Relationship has two boxes, marked S and B, which can be checked, X'd, or filled-in to indicate if that element is Stressed or Broken, respectively.

A Stressed element can still be used as normal. If the same Attribute, Skill, or Relationship would be Stressed a second time, it is then Broken. Broken elements can't be used again until they are Healed. A Broken element that is Healed becomes Stressed and can be used as normal, but risks becoming Broken again.

The narrative fiction of the scene should reflect the way the Active Player's Hero becomes Stressed. Maybe they're forced to run across broken glass without shoes; they manage to survive, but now they have to spend a few moments picking the glass out of their feet. Maybe a Hero thought about their daughter, who they've never had a good relationship with, for mental encouragement, but then failed to escape from the cultists. Now they're reeling emotionally, thinking how they've proven once again that they aren't fit to be a parent and their kid is right for not wanting to spend time with them.

For every 1 in a Dice Pool, something must be Stressed. An element may be Stressed twice from the same Dice Pool roll, causing it to become Broken immediately. Stress is never applied to elements which were not used to build a Dice Pool, even if the number of 1s exceeds the amount of Stress which can be assigned. If the Active Player rolls a 1 while Leveraging their Hero's Achilles' Heel, that 1 only generates one Stress, not two.

HEALING

Because this is an action movie, the Hero will never die unless their controlling player wants them to. Instead, the Stress and Breaking mechanic shows the bumps, bruises, and emotional distress they're feeling.

But no matter how Stressed or Broken they get, they will find a way to push on. That's what the Healing mechanic is for. When a Hero receives Healing, they can remove Stress from two elements, or move one element from Broken to Stressed.

Healing can happen in a number of ways.

1. Each Hero gets one Healing during the Response/Reset scene between each Act.
2. If an Active Player gets two or more 12 results in a Dice Pool, they may give one Healing to any Hero in that scene, including their own. This Healing would be in addition to any other bonuses granted by rolling a 12.

3. If any player drops an amazing one-liner that cracks up the entire table, every Hero gets one Healing. Does this make sense narratively? No, but laughing at the table is a good thing. If a player makes the table laugh, they get rewarded.

ALTERING THE DICE POOL RESULTS

There are several ways to modify a Dice Pool. Two have already been mentioned: the Achilles' Heel, which allows the Active Player to roll two additional dice, and the Heroic Trait, which can be Leveraged to reroll some of the dice. Here are some additional ways to alter the roll results before they are considered final.

TWELVES EXPLODE!

If a 12 is rolled in a Dice Pool, it counts as two Successes instead of one. However, the Active Player may choose to reroll any 12, adding the new roll to the current Dice Pool result. This might result in a Setback, reducing the net Success of the roll, or it might result in another Success, providing further progress toward the current Obstacle. It may even result in another 12, which would generate two more Successes and allow the Active Player to repeat the process.

HEROIC HIGH FIVE

If the player doesn't wish to reroll a 12 and doesn't need or want to use it for Healing, they can "bank" them. This is a very special rule, and creates the only time a player may roll dice when they are not the Active Player. An Active Player may bank as many 12s as they wish, but may only roll one of their banked 12s at a time, though multiple players may roll banked 12s on the same Active Player's turn.

When rolled this way, these 12s are called a Heroic High Five, and represent when two or more Heroes work together. Much like Relationships, this could be because they are in the same scene together, or an emotional or inspirational push. The player should inform the Active Player when they wish to roll their Heroic High Five, and should explain how they are assisting the Active Player in the scene.

The Heroic High Five die is special: all Heroic High Five roll results of 1-11 count as one Success, meaning it's impossible to add a Setback to a Dice Pool when using a Heroic High Five die. Heroic High Fives will ALWAYS add at least one Success to the Dice Pool.

12s still count as two Successes, and still explode. However, players can't bank a new die from a Heroic High Five, so the only option is to add two Successes and then roll it again. It is still treated as a Heroic High Five die, and can still continue to explode on a result of 12.

Teamwork makes the dream work!

THE NEEDLE DROP

Another classic trope of action movies is that banger of a song (or, sometimes, a hauntingly slow cover of an old-school banger) that plays over the action of a particular scene.

Each player can name drop the perfect song to be playing over the current action, once per game. It doesn't have to be the Active Player; any player can do a Needle Drop, at any time. If the group agrees that the song would be perfect at this moment, the Active Player can turn one Setback into a Blank. If any player actually begins to sing the song (and it's better if everyone joins in), then the Active Player can turn one Setback into a Success.

It's up to the group how much of the song must be sung to qualify, and if no one wants to sing, playing the song at the table is sufficient.

HERO STOLE MY BIKE

"Sorry Kid, end-of-the-world-type non-sense ... again!"

PUSHED TO THE LIMIT

Sometimes something's just too much for one person - or it certainly seems that way, until that one person manages to do that thing. But the extra effort used to push through often takes its toll, and that Hero needs a nap. That is being Pushed to the Limit.

Once per game, the Active Player can choose to turn a 1 result on a die in their current Dice Pool into a 12. This 12 counts as two Successes and can be spent as a resource, like any other 12. However, the effort the Hero mustered to get this Heroic Success also results in their going unconscious. This means that player will no longer take a turn as Active Player until the end of the current Act. An unconscious Hero can benefit from Healing as usual, but Healing does not revive an unconscious Hero.

Be sure to describe how the Hero managed to pull through when all hope was lost, and now needs to lie down for a little bit. Also, keep in mind that the unconscious Hero doesn't disappear from the scene. They're there in body, if not in spirit, and as long as their controlling player agrees, the other players can incorporate their body into their turns, possibly ensuring they get out safely. Maybe as a prop?

HEROIC SACRIFICE

Normally, Heroes in *Action 12 Cinema* can't die; however, the Active Player may choose to have their Hero die by making a Heroic Sacrifice. In exchange for this Heroic Sacrifice, they can change any single die result in their current Dice Pool to a 12, which works like any other 12.

In addition, they get a number of Heroic High Five dice equal to the number of other players. For the remainder of the game, they can use one of those Heroic High Five dice by including a detail on how their sacrifice helped the Active Player in their current effort. They may only use one of these Heroic High Five dice per player.

THE SECRET TO GETTING THE MOST OUT OF THE GAME

Action 12 Cinema is a weird hybrid game that walks the line between storytelling and roleplaying while also being GM-less. Over the game's development, I have found that this can be extremely fun, but it can also be confusing - more so to experienced roleplayers who aren't accustomed to taking turns with narrative control. In my experience, seasoned players are more likely to want to interject their characters into the scene, and roleplay or roll dice as part of the action, when someone else is the Active Player.

That isn't how this game works. The interjection can, and does, but only the Active Player rolls dice (outside of the Heroic High Five). A key to understanding this dance is that when you aren't the Active Player, you don't need to roll dice to allow your Hero to have an effect on the action. Just let the Active Player know what you want to do, and they can weave your suggestions into their narration and roleplay. If you want to throw a rock to distract an approaching guard, you do that, as long as the Active Player says you did.

Here are some other concepts I've found that can help smooth out some of the rough edges of how abstracted Obstacles work.

BREAKING OBSTACLES INTO PARTS

One of the ways to really make **Action 12 Cinema** sing is to work with your table to break down your Obstacles into smaller pieces, so that Incremental Successes are building the fiction to the Complete Success resolution.

If you're dealing with an Obstacle of Fire, for example, you could describe grabbing a fire extinguisher and using it to fight the fire directly. Each Incremental Success means you've made progress, and the fire is getting smaller and smaller. There's absolutely nothing wrong with that, but you could also describe your Hero realizing the fire suppression system isn't activating, so they rush off to find a fire extinguisher.

You could roll at this moment, and Success could mean that you find a fire extinguisher, so of course the fire is now closer to being put out. The next Active Player may narrate how they get into the control room and are using hacking skills to reactivate the sabotaged fire suppression system. An Incremental Success could be reaching that area, or reaching the area and accessing the system, or reaching that area, accessing the system, and getting some, but not all, sprinklers to turn on. Each player in turn can really explore how their Hero is dealing with their part of the issue.

By breaking the Obstacle into smaller chunks, you can account for Incremental Successes in the fiction and build to a satisfying conclusion. Pretty much any Obstacle can be broken down in this way, based on the fiction already established and the genre/BBEG/plot of the story you're in.

AN EXTENDED EXAMPLE: A CHASE

Knowing when to interrupt your narration to build and roll your Dice Pool can make a huge difference in how the story plays out. Let's take an extended look at how a Chase might look, depending on when you roll your Dice Pool.

If you've watched even half of the bad (but fun!) action movies I have, then you're probably familiar with this type of scene. It's the beginning of a chase and the bad guy is getting away, but the Hero doesn't have a vehicle to pursue in. They pull out their badge and gun, and stand in the middle of the road to commandeer a civilian's vehicle.

This usually involves kicking the civilian out of their car, but occasionally they refuse to get out, and sometimes the civilian drives.

Now in hot pursuit, our Hero drives through a busy intersection or two - against the traffic light - and narrowly avoids getting hit by cross-traffic. There is often a wreck that occurs because of this chase, but it's in our Hero's rear-view mirror.

The chase continues until both vehicles are on the highway. Perhaps the cars ram into one another, each trying to run the other off the road. Finally, one vehicle forces the other to plow into a barricade of water-filled barrels at the exit ramp. The chase ends in a plume of water!

This is exactly the sort of scene that could - and should - happen in an ***Action 12 Cinema*** game. But we have a lot of options on when we could roll our Dice Pool, and each place gives us different options on how to interpret Incremental Successes, or even Critical Failures.

EXAMPLES
#1: Which Vehicle Do You Get?

Perhaps our Active Player decides to roll very early in this scene, and rolls just as they are attempting to commandeer a vehicle. In this case, a success could mean that the vehicle they manage to stop is a muscle car or a street bike. Either could give our Hero a great chance to catch up with our fleeing bad guy. A failure could mean that the only vehicle they manage to use is an old beat-up pickup truck, or maybe even a Vespa-style scooter.

#2: Running the Red Lights

Let's assume our Hero has gotten a very fast street bike, and they're weaving in and out of traffic after our fleeing bad guy. They decide to roll as they are trying to jet through a red light and avoid the cross-traffic. A success here has the Hero successfully weaving through traffic, and the wrecks happen in their wake. A failure could mean that our Hero doesn't make it through. Their fast vehicle is damaged, forcing them to get into yet another vehicle, and this time it is a scooter or old station wagon.

#3: The Crash!

Let's assume our Active Player waits to roll until around the time they're narrating how the two cars are bumping into one another on the highway. A success here (especially a Complete Success roll) could mean that the Hero manages to slam the bad guy's car into those water barrels. A failure might mean our Hero's car ends up in the barrels instead.

As you can see in each case, the Active Player's choice of when to interrupt their narration to build and roll their Dice Pool gives a variety of options for interpreting the results.

Though it isn't the primary purpose of GM-less games, I think this example also highlights how playing in GM-less games can help build skills for running a more traditional RPG as a GM. Figuring out all the ways you can choose to roll, and playing with the multiple ways the results can be interpreted, is very much what a GM does in a traditional RPG. Whether you have yet to try your hand at GMing, or just want to improve your improv skills, playing **Action 12 Cinema** - as well as other GM-less games - can be a beneficial way of challenging and training yourself.

BUT WHAT IF WE HAVE A TEAM OF HEROES IN THIS CHASE?

We are only following one Hero in the Chase example above, so let's modify it to show how a Chase might play out with a team of Heroes.

Active Player 1 rolls early, and uses their Success to commandeer a muscle car and give chase.

Active Player 2 is already on a motorbike. They run interference by following behind our other Hero, and use their bike to keep some bad-guy minions from shooting out the tires of our first Hero's car.

Active Player 3 is using their computer wizardry to fly a drone overhead and relay directions to the chasing Hero so they can catch up with the bad guy, despite not being able to see them at the moment. Maybe they're also hacking the traffic lights so our Hero has all greens and our fleeing bad guy is running red lights.

These are a few options of how a team of Heroes could work together in subsequent Active Player turns to break the Chase Obstacle into smaller pieces that give each player a way to help build toward the conclusion.

One final reminder: this Chase could reach Complete Success, but in the narration the bad guy still gets away. Maybe the Heroes were chasing the wrong car the whole time. The bad guy may have set up a decoy, or even switched cars mid-chase without being seen.

ADJUSTING DIFFICULTY

The rules for overcoming Obstacles rely on Successes generated from a Dice Pool. At the standard setting, Successes are generated with any result of eight or higher, with 12s counting as two Successes.

There may be some reasons to adjust this threshold. In a more lighthearted game, the Success threshold could be lowered to seven, or even six. For a more intense story - perhaps a horror story - you could raise it to nine, or even ten.

You could change the threshold based on what part of the story you're in. Each subsequent Act raises the threshold - the Act One threshold is seven, it moves to eight in Act Two, and for the final showdown in Act Three it's nine.

PRECARIOUS LEDGE

This should be a group decision, and known before the game begins. I highly suggest you start with the standard threshold of eight for the first game before moving it around.

It's important to note that the threshold should never change based on who's rolling or what they're trying to do. Part of the fun is that any sort of wild idea or action has an equal chance of success. Only the dice results decide if something works or not.

CORNER CASES

On average, it should take four or five Active Player turns to complete an Obstacle. You may occasionally run into a situation where one player rolls extremely well and clears an entire Obstacle on their own, or only one or two players get to be an Active Player. While this is exciting for the one(s) rolling, it might be a bit of a letdown for everyone else. Here are some suggestions for these extreme corner cases.

OVER WAY TOO SOON

If a player rolls so well that they've overcome an Obstacle quickly, take the opportunity to bring everyone in. The rules say that the Obstacle is defeated at the end of your turn, but it doesn't dictate how or why. Let every player take a short turn narrating as if it was their turn. Let everyone feed off the success and play as if they had also rolled well.

THIS IS TAKING FOREVER

Sometimes the dice just aren't kind. A bad roll at a bad time can extend a single Obstacle past the point of being fun. Normally a bad roll just adds to the fun and excitement, but everything has its limits. If a single roll - or a series of bad rolls - is taking things from fun and exciting to frustrating, the players as a whole can agree to have a Rewrite, which is where a new draft of the movie was written and the current activities have been written out. Just add a quick line where a character says, "You know, I'm still not sure how we managed to get out of that situation alive, but I'm glad we did." and end that current Obstacle.

ALTERNATE MODES OF PLAY

VILLAIN MODE

Action 12 Cinema is about telling B-Grade Action Movie stories, and for the most part those are about Heroes, but you can play a game where you're the Villains if you want to. Everything works pretty much the same, except instead of trying to overcome Obstacles, you are using those Obstacles to further your own ends. A Fight! becomes you or your minions attacking civilians or the military. Finding the Missing Person could become kidnapping a person or stealing something. Just put a slight twist on the narration to make it clear how you're trying to do the thing versus stop the thing.

SINGLE HERO MODE

It's very common for action movies to focus on a single protagonist or Hero. If you want to play *Action 12 Cinema* as a single player storytelling game, perhaps as a journaling game where you write out the script as you go, you can. You can also have multiple players controlling the same Hero. The players will build their single Hero as a group, and then during each Active Player turn they get to control the Hero's actions, while the other players play Supporting Characters as needed. I suggest you either create a few more Supporting Characters than usual, or assume some of the Supporting Characters work more like side-kicks and are in almost all the scenes with our main Hero.

TRAITOR MODE

In one very memorable playtest, I had a player decide in Act Two to reveal themselves as having been the Villain all along. It actually made sense in the game, but we had to make up rules on the fly, as this was the first time it had come up. I'm still not 100% sure on this one, but what we did was just have that character become the Villain, that Player got to narrate and roleplay them on their turn but they didn't roll any dice to try and further their own schemes/ends. The dice mechanic doesn't work well for confrontation, but if you want to try something else, let me know what you come up with!

TROPE DESCRIPTIONS AND EXPLANATIONS:

10-Minute Retirement: A hero will give up in the middle of some calamity, saying something like, "I'm too old for this," or "Somebody else might be able to do this, but not me." Shortly after, they have an epiphany where they come out of that retirement, and announce they are back.

Absurdly Sharp Blade: A weapon with a blade sharper than it has any reason to be, other than for comedic or dramatic effect.

Acquired Poison Immunity: The development of immunity to a particular drug or poison by taking small doses for a long time.

Action Dad: The moment when a father figure who appears to be out of the picture or uninvolved becomes protective and helpful when the family is in danger.

Action Dress Rip: When an Action Girl finds herself in a dress, she'll rip it before going into a situation that actually requires action.

Action Girl: A female badass. Either one that presents that way at the beginning of the movie, or someone who comes into her own as the movie progresses.

BAD GUY BAR

LANTERN SHOULD BE BRIGHTEST IN DARK ROOM — TOO "ON THE NOSE?"

Action Insurance Gag: The moment when someone asks someone if they have insurance just before something destructive occurs.

Action Mom: A mother figure who keeps her role as savior and raises the children. She's a real badass mother.

Action Film, Quiet Drama Scene: A quiet moment between one or more characters in the middle of an otherwise action-filled story.

Acoustic License: When characters are able to talk and be heard clearly despite being in an obviously loud and chaotic environment.

Adrenaline Makeover: A series of events which leads a character, who begins by appearing shy or timid, to become increasingly badass and attractive the further they fall into the action.

After-Action Healing Drama: A quiet scene after a big action moment where characters are able to get treatment for their wounds, likely while hashing out tension between themselves.

Air Vent Passageway: When heroes find themselves trapped in a room with all doors and windows locked, the quickest exit is always through the ventilation duct.

All I have Left is This!: Heroes or villains are forced to use an apparently less-effective weapon that is inexplicably more powerful than any other weapon they could use.

Almost Out of Oxygen: Imminent death by suffocation to raise the stakes.

Always a Bigger Fish: Where the Heroes are saved from a scary monster by a larger, scarier monster.

An Ass-Kicking Christmas: When your action movie overlaps with the Christmas holiday.

And Mission Control Rejoiced: When Mission Control breaks into cheering due to the actions of the Heroes, often when accomplishing something thought impossible or surviving something expected to be deadly.

And They Said [blank] Was a Waste of Time: A character has acquired a much-needed Skill through a hobby or interest.

Backing into Danger: A character keeps their eyes open for danger, only to back right into it.

Bad Habits: When Heroes or villains dress up as religious figures (usually Catholic nuns) for comedic or dramatic effect.

Bad-Guy Bar: The place where the bad guys hang out to plot their nefarious deeds.

Badass Driver: A Hero who can drive anything better than anyone else. Doing things with a vehicle lesser people would believe impossible (and probably are, outside of this movie).

Banging for Help: A trapped character does this to attract attention from people outside.

Bar Slide: When a bartender slides a mug, cup, or shot glass down the bar. It's often caught, but sometimes not. Variation: Someone gets thrown on the bar during a fight, then dragged down it and off the end.

Barrier-Busting Blow: A super-strong character or monster punches through a door or wall to reach the victim on the other side.

Bathroom Break-Out: When a Hero craftily makes their way into what appears to be a secure bathroom, but manages to escape through the window, an air vent, or some other very unlikely exit.

Beast in the Maze: When a vicious beast lurks within a maze our Heroes must travel through. No matter what precautions the Heroes take, the beast will arrive or be found at the dramatically appropriate time.

Big, Heroic Run: The Hero or Heroes have to run very fast to save someone, escape someone, deliver critical info, or some other reason. They are often navigating a dangerous course at the same time.

Bloodless Carnage: No matter how deadly a battle is, you won't see entrance wounds, exit wounds, or any blood at all anywhere on or near anyone on screen.

Bluff the Impostor: You think someone is an impostor, so you say something to them with an erroneous fact, and see if they react to it.

Body Bag Trick: When a character hides in a body bag and is wheeled into or out of a hospital or other facility, then gets out and does their mission.

Bodyguard Babes: When the BBEG's elite protectors are exclusively female warriors.

Bombproof Appliance: When the hero hides in a bathtub or fridge to avoid a bomb that is going to go off indoors.

Bookcase Passage: A secret passage is hidden behind a bookcase, triggered by the removal or manipulation of a book in a bookcase.

Boomerang Comeback: The thrown weapon that you thought missed its target is coming back around for a second go.

Bottled Heroic Reserve: When a Hero imbibes something (drug, alcohol, super serum) and gets back on their feet, ready for more action.

Bound and Gagged: When someone - usually not our Heroes, but someone the villains have kidnapped - is bound and gagged to put them in danger (death trap) or keep them out of the way and quiet while the villains prepare for the Hero(es) to come and rescue them.

Breaking the Bonds: Heroes showing off their power by busting out of chains, ropes, or similar restraints.

Break Out the Museum Piece: When the modern weaponry or equipment has been destroyed or taken away, the Heroes resort to outdated stuff to do the job.

Bullet Catch: A Hero shows off their abilities by catching a thrown or fired weapon.

Bulletproof Human Shield: Grab a nearby mook and let them absorb bullets while you head for safety or move closer to your enemy.

Bulletproof Furniture: Hiding behind furniture during a gunfight, when bullets should rip right through them but don't.

Cable-Car Action Sequence: Action sequence occurring on one or more cable cars high in the air.

Cacophony Cover-Up: When you need to time your stealth with a louder sound you create or wait for.

Cavalry Betrayal: When a person or group appears to be coming to rescue or aid our Heroes, only to find they are the villains, or are working for them.

Car Cushion: Falling from a great height but surviving by falling onto a car, into a garbage truck, or something similar.

Catch a Falling Star: When a Hero is falling from a great height and is caught by someone and saved, sometimes via a vehicle, even if the act of catching them should have also been deadly.

Caught in a Snare: Our Heroes fall into a trap while traversing a jungle or forest. Either netted together or hanging upside down by an ankle, they must find a way out or wait till they are let down by whomever set the snare.

Carnival of Killers: When a series of assassins, either seeking a bounty or having been hired by the villain, goes after the Hero.

Cave Mouth: When a cave mouth looks like an actual mouth, or when a cave turns out to BE the mouth of a humongous monster.

Ceiling Cling: A character avoids pursuit or detection by hanging from the ceiling of the room or hallway.

Ceiling Crash: When a Hero crashes through a ceiling or skylight and into the midst of their enemies.

Ceiling Smash: When a combatant gets hit so hard during a fight that they fly up, smash against the ceiling, and then fall back down, usually resulting in only superficial wounds.

Check the Visor: Our Heroes are able to get into a strange vehicle and escape, thanks to the owner leaving the keys readily available.

Chekhov's Exhibit: When an item that will ultimately be part of the action is on display as part of an exhibit. Often shown much earlier that it comes into play as foreshadowing.

Cigar-Fuse Lighting: When a villain uses their cigar to light the fuse on explosives.

Clifftop Caterwauling: When a character stands on the edge of a cliff and cries out in victory, grief,or as a challenge to the villain,

Climbing the Cliffs of Insanity: When the Hero must climb an absurdly tall cliff or building to proceed.

Climb, Slip, Hang, Climb: Whenever a character has to climb without safety gear, they are bound to slip or grab a ledge that breaks off so they will be hanging on one hand. The character will then inevitably look down, take a deep breath, and resume climbing.

Clipboard of Authority: A person with a clipboard, acting like an authority figure, can get into just about anywhere.

Clockwork Prediction: Someone predicts something comical someone is going to do within the next few moments.

Cobweb Jungle: When an area, usually subterranean, is filled with large quantities of cobwebs. Often used as shorthand that no one has been in this area for a long time.

Colossus Climb: A small(er) character damages a bigger character by climbing its body to attack a vulnerable spot.

Concert Climax: When the climax of the movie takes place around some big public event, such as a concert, performance, sporting event, or similar public gathering that the Heroes, for whatever reason, have been brought to.

Contract on the Hitman: When the Heroes are suddenly hunted by the same organization they work(ed) for. Often due to corruption or mistaken information.

Convenient Enemy Base: If the Heroes crash-land or shipwreck while on a mission against a powerful enemy, they will almost always wash up very close to that enemy's hidden headquarters.

Convenient Escape Boat: When escaping anywhere near a body of water, there will be a boat leaving the harbor the Heroes can jump onto.

Conveniently Placed Sharp Thing: Someone is tied up, but the bad guys leave something sharp in the room that the victim can use to cut themselves free.

WEAPONIZED CAR

← Close-up insert; blurred edge a la split-field diopter

Conveniently Timed Attack from Behind: A Hero or other character is helpless and about to be killed, when their attacker is taken out just in time by a Hero who had gotten behind them without being seen by anyone.

Cool and Unusual Punishment: A torture scene where the torture is as unusual as it is evil.

Cut the Red Wire. No, Wait, the Blue Wire: A bomb is about to explode unless you cut the right color-coded wire, often choosing a different one at the last moment.

Cyanide Pill: Zealous bad guy minions will never talk!

Danger with a Deadline: When the Heroes (or villains) have a strict time limit on their plan to be implemented or defeated.

Darkened Building Shootout: A shootout occurs in a darkened room or building, with the results not apparent until the lights are turned back on.

Dead Foot Leadfoot: The driver of a vehicle is killed; immediately, his foot gets stuck on the gas pedal, causing the car to speed out of control.

Dead Man's Switch: A device rigged to detonate if a pressure switch is released, usually when the person using it dies. Generally used as a protection to keep that person alive.

Dead Man's Trigger Finger: A character wildly fires an automatic weapon immediately after being shot.

Deadly Gas: A situation where the Heroes must outlast or pass through a space filled with lethal gas (which is often green).

Death Course: A gauntlet filled with enemies and/or booby traps that the Hero character has to pass through.

Death Trap: Where the villains use an overly elaborate death machine instead of just killing the Heroes. They often leave assuming the Heroes are now dead.

Decoy Hiding Place: An obvious hiding place is made visible to the pursuer, while the pursued actually escapes via some other means.

Deep Cover Agent: A person thought to be an innocent turns out to be deep undercover. Are they the villain, or an ally?

Delivery Guy Infiltration: A Character poses as a delivery person to get past guards, or to get someone to open a door.

Desperate Object Catch: All will be lost if the falling object isn't caught in time.

Diner Brawl: One or more characters are trying to have a nice meal when an inexplicably aggressive diner patron decides to pick a fight. The patron might even have one or more inexplicably aggressive friends backing them up. This will result in an altercation of some sort, despite the character's best efforts to avoid a fight.

Dirt Forcefield: When, despite everything they've been through, our Heroes emerge on the other side of battle with hardly any dirt or damage to their clothing - unless they are sexy, and the damage to their clothing makes it slightly more revealing.

Disaster-Dodging Doggo: The dog always survives, no matter the odds.

Dish Dash: A character has to dash madly around a room, catching stacks of falling breakable items before they hit the floor and smash.

Disney Death: When a character is thought to have died in order to elicit a reaction, only to reveal they weren't actually dead after all.

Diving into the Truck: When a Hero dives into an already moving vehicle in an attempt to make a hasty retreat, often only getting partly inside as they drive away.

Dog Pile of Doom: Where large numbers of mooks bring a Hero down by jumping on top of them and physically dragging them to the ground.

Don't You Give Up on Me!: A Hero appears to die, but is revived in some dramatic manner.

Dressing as the Enemy: Where the Hero dresses up in a face-concealing suit of armor stolen from the enemy to infiltrate their base.

Driving into a Truck: Escaping pursuit by driving your vehicle into a larger one (most often a car into a truck) while both are in motion.

Drool Hello: The first inkling that a monster is above you? That yucky liquid splashing over your shoulders...

Dungeon Bypass: Where Heroes just blast through or over the complicated maze or trial that the villain has set up, rather than actually solving it.

Durable Deathtrap: The ruins are ancient, but damn if those giant guillotine blades aren't as sharp as the day they were made!

Dye or Die: When a character makes a drastic hair change as a disguise, often changing the color, but sometimes by shaving or wearing a wig.

Ejection Seat: A seat that is rigged to forcefully eject someone from a vehicle. Try not to accidentally push the button.

Emergency Cargo Dump: When characters throw away objects to decrease weight or ballast. This may be to prevent a faltering plane from crashing or a leaky boat from sinking, or to gain speed over a pursuer.

Emergency Stash: When a Hero has a stash of gear, guns, money, or documents they can retrieve. Often at a bank, rental lockers, or a safe house.

Empty Elevator: Will the Hero/villain/monster be in the elevator when it opens? Of course not! They're hiding somewhere nearby, ready to kick ass.

Empty Quiver: When our Hero runs out of ammo, just to have to dramatically fist fight the final enemy.

Enemy Rising Behind: Someone (or something) hostile is coming into view from behind and below.

Enhance!: When the characters are able to zoom in on an image well beyond realistic capabilities and find enough details or clues to lead them to the next scene.

Exotic Weapon Supremacy: If a character uses an unusual weapon, it indicates that they're more badass than everyone else.

Exploding Fish Tanks: If an aquarium is shown at any point, the aquarium will inevitably be destroyed.

Exposition Diagram: A diagram is set up to explain the upcoming plan.

Facing the Bullets One-Liner: A character has one last thing to say before they die, which is the equivalent of, "Go screw yourself," or, "This isn't over yet," or otherwise demonstrating their continued defiance toward and disdain for their killers.

Fast Roping: When a group of Heroes join into the action of a battle by quickly rappelling down from above.

Feed the Bad Beastie: When Heroes or allies are fed to a monster… or when the BBEG tries it, anyway.

Feed the Good Beastie: When a Hero can make an ally out of what appears to be an evil beast by offering it food, or otherwise making a friendly connection.

Ferris Wheel of Doom: If there is a Ferris Wheel in a shot, it will become unmoored at some point and begin rolling through the scene.

Fighter-Launching Sequence: When a bunch of fighters (planes, spaceships, mechs) go into battle, you always have to see them taking off first.

Flamethrower Backfire: What's the best way to beat a guy with a flamethrower? Blow up the fuel tank!

Flaming Emblem: When our Hero or villain takes time out of their busy schedule to leave a message or their emblem in flammable liquid, so that when, by happenstance, someone throws down a match or otherwise ignites it, and their emblem is set ablaze.

Flynning: An overly-choreographed sword duel that looks amazing on camera.

Foe-Tossing Charge: Where a character barrels toward a target and tosses away anyone who gets in the way without a glance.

Forced To Fight: Combatants are forced by The Powers That Be to brawl, box, or otherwise fight - sometimes to the death.

Forging Scene: A scene dedicated to forging a kickass weapon, or something equally as bad-ass

Futile Hand Reach: A moment where a character sees something that is about to happen but is powerless to stop it, and so raises their hand out toward the action. Often accompanied by a shout of, "NOOOOO!"

Gasoline Dowsing: When a character gets out a gas can to douse something in gasoline, then light it on fire.

Get the Gun Already!: Two or more characters fight over a weapon during a fight scene that manages to stay just out of reach.

Giant Foot of Stomping: A big foot comes out of nowhere and stomps someone to death.

Giving the Sword to the Noob: When there is a brand-new or singularly powerful weapon that, if wielded by the right person, can turn the tide of battle. Too bad we can't get it to the right person, so we'll give it to "this person" and hope for the best.

Gladiator Games: When people are forced to fight each other or monsters/creatures for the entertainment of others - usually the villain.

Goggles Do Something Unusual: Eyewear that does something other than what their mundane design purpose is.

Government Agency of Fiction: A government agency that is working for or against our Heroes, usually with an overly complicated name that can be shortened into an acronym (see S.H.I.E.L.D. or SPECTRE).

Grave Robbing: A grave must be dug up for some purpose, including taking something buried with the body.

Great Escape: When a large portion of the plot revolves around planning for, and then executing, an escape. Especially if the place is considered escape-proof.

Gunpoint Banter: When two characters have their guns aimed at one another, ready to shoot, but decide to have a conversation instead.

Hallway Fight: A fight that takes place in a corridor. The fighters are more-or-less forced to go in one direction, while the narrow and cramped quarters force them into a more claustrophobic battle.

Hands Off My Fluffy!: Where the Heroes attack a monster who looks like it's accosting a girl, when it turns out the monster is the girl's pet.

Hardcore Parkour: Getting from point A to point B in a non-traditional fashion.

Harmless Freezing: A character is frozen solid, and then unfreezes with no adverse effects.

Hassle-free Hotwire: When a character surprises everyone by being able to hotwire any vehicle in seconds.

Hastily Made Prop: When forced to improvise an essential prop for a costume or device, it works perfectly.

Hero Stole My Bike: A Hero in a hurry grabs somebody else's car or bike to aid in a chase scene.

"He's Right Behind Me, Isn't He?": A character is talking about someone, only to realize that person is right behind them and has overhead what they said.

"Hey, Catch!": A character who throws something to another character to make them catch it, often a distraction.

"Hey, Wait!": When a character appears to clear a checkpoint or get past guards, only to be called back after expressing a sigh of relief and facing additional scrutiny.

"Hey, You!" Haymaker: Tap your opponent on the back, and when they turn around, you punch them in the face.

High-Speed Chase: A high speed chase, often through a congested area.

Hitchhiking Heroes: When our Heroes are forced to hit the road without wheels of their own, but, as luck would have it, a well-timed good Samaritan will give them a ride, and even put their own lives at risk to protect them against detection.

Hollywood Acid: When acid is used in an action film and only does exactly what the plot needs it to.

Hollywood CB: When a CB allows for two-way communication, even when it's clear the users are not depressing or releasing the mic button as necessary for that conversation to take place.

Hollywood Fire: When fire behaves in an unusual way because that's what the fire needs to do for the movie.

Honor Among Thieves: At times, the only thing a down-on-their-luck Hero can count on is the criminal family they knew before.

Hotwire: Heroes can hotwire any vehicle with just two wires.

Human Chess: Nothing says evil overlord louder than using human pieces in your chess game, and having the pieces die when they're taken off the board.

Hunting the Most Dangerous Game: Where the villains formally hunt the Heroes, civilians, or Supporting Characters.

Inconveniently Timed Guard: The Heroes have just finished their infiltration, but a guard sees them on their way out and sounds the alarm.

I Need No Ladders: Any time a Hero eschews the obvious ladder or stairs for some more action oriented, if circuitous, route.

If You're So Evil, Eat This Kitten: The bad guys challenge someone (usually the Hero pretending to be a Bad Guy) to do something evil to prove their evilness.

Imminent Danger Clue: The moment when a Hero notices some seemingly insignificant detail that warns them of imminent danger, but it's already too late.

Implausible Fencing Powers: Where swordsmen can do insane things with their swords, like deflecting bullets or cutting clothes to pieces without touching skin.

Impressive Pyrotechnics: A fireball or other explosion that looks amazing on camera, but makes no sense in regard to what caused the explosion.

Impossible Mission Collapse: We hear all the planning for an elaborate, high-risk plan concocted by the good guys, and then it never gets past step one.

Improbable Cover: When a character leaps behind something to escape an explosion, ducks to avoid a rolling wall of flame, or closes a door on an avalanche.

Improvised Parachute: What a character uses to slow a great fall when a real parachute is not available.

Improvised Zipline: When a character really needs to rappel down a building but doesn't have a rope, they'll improvise one.

Indy Escape: Outrunning some non-stop object rushing towards you. With no way to avoid it - just keep running straight and then jump to safety at the last moment.

Indy Hat Roll: Any version of rolling, diving, sliding under a door that is closing, with enough time left to reach in and grab something that can't be left behind.

Inevitable Waterfall: If a character is drifting on a raft or logs along a river, they will soon learn of an impending waterfall.

Instant Knots: Where Heroes can make a rope, whip, chain, or grappling hook wrap itself around distant objects securely.

Instrument of Murder: Any version of a weapon concealed inside of a musical instrument or case, including the instrument itself being used as a weapon.

Involuntary Group Split: When something occurs to split our group of Heroes and they must go on separately.

Juggle-Fu: Someone can throw an object in the air, perform some action sequence while it is airborne, then catch it on its way down.

Just a Kid: When a young Hero is dismissed time and time again by other Heroes or villains because of their age.

Katanas Are Just Better: When you need a sword, you need a katana. If there is ever an issue of who is better with a sword or who has the better sword, the katana wins.

Keep Away: The game of tossing an object around in a group to keep it away from someone else.

Kidnapped from Behind: An abduction that occurs when the victim is taken from a group, but no one notices because they were standing alone or at the back of the line.

Kinda Busy Here: When a cell phone rings at an inconvenient time, like when you're in a gunfight.

Kissus Interruptus: After some "will they/won't they" build up, two Heroes are about to kiss when they're interrupted, and have to jump apart and awkwardly explain that nothing is happening.

Kitchen Chase: The Hero runs through an active kitchen to escape the bad guys.

Latex Perfection: A latex mask so perfect that it is impossible to tell the wearer from the person they are impersonating until the moment it's removed.

Let's Fight Like Gentlemen: No matter how much they hate each other, the two opponents will stick to the rules in their fight.

Life-or-Limb Decision: A situation where a hero is forced to make a terrible choice—they must remove or lose one of their appendages in order to escape with their life.

Line in the Sand: Can be a situation where a commander is calling for volunteers and the Heroes step forward to volunteer (or everyone else steps back), or a literal line on the ground which our Heroes must not let the enemies cross in order to be victorious.

Locking MacGyver in the Store Cupboard: When the good guys get locked in a cell, all of the equipment that they need to escape is in the cell with them.

Luck-Based Search Technique: The only way to find the secret passage is by sheer luck.

Man on Fire: Classic stunt where someone walks around briefly while on fire.

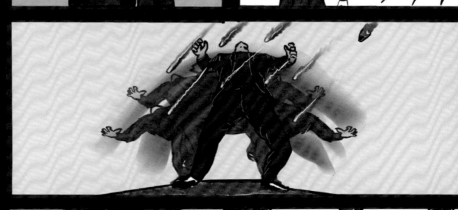

Marked Bullet: A bullet with special markings or words on it, often the name of someone a character wants dead.

Mexican Standoff: A standoff featuring more than two opponents or factions, often with everyone holding a weapon in each hand pointed and different opponents or factions. Doves flapping nearby are a plus.

Midair Repair: Where a malfunctioning, falling aircraft must be fixed by the mechanic in midair before it hits the ground.

Mirror Scare: A Hero closes a medicine cabinet and there's suddenly something behind them in the mirror.

Mission Briefing: The big, "Let's go over the mission to see just how impossible it is before we go and do it," scene.

Monumental Damage: When large-scale damage is being done, it will always include recognizable buildings or monuments.

Morse Code: Using low-tech communication to avoid bad guy detection.

My Name is Inigo Montoya: When one of the combatants will introduce themselves unprompted just before a duel, so the other person knows who is about to beat them, or to elicit a reaction if they are famous.

Nerf Arm: Any logically less-than-lethal weapon which ends up being just as effective as its "real" equivalent.

Nitro Express: Hauling unstable explosives over dangerous terrain.

No Collateral Damage: When you blow up the giant monster/enemy base, it should cause untold damage to the places around it, but we never see such damage.

No One Will Follow This: Jumping from high cliff into water to get away.

No OSHA Compliance: Bases and complexes have all kinds of insanely dangerous walkways and areas, because they're cool.

Non-Fatal Explosions: Explosions don't cause concussion damage from the shockwave or rip you up with shrapnel... they just give you a little push.

Not Dead Yet: A bad guy who looks to be dead isn't, and pops back up.

Not in This for Your Revolution: Despite the colossal stakes at play in the fate of the universe, a Hero is only in this for themselves and how they can personally benefit. At least, that's what they say.

Now It's My Turn: Where one character survives what has been built up as a nasty attack, grins, and unleashes a counterattack.

Ominous Walk: A villain, or anti-hero, will have an enemy at their mercy and instead of immediately shooting them, they'll slowly walk towards them.

One at a Time!: When the bad guys are waiting for their turn to attack.

One-Dimensional Thinking: When characters are being chased by something and, despite a sharp left or right turn being the easiest and obvious way out of danger, they will continue to run straight ahead.

"Open!" Says Me: When met with an unyielding door lock, one of the Heroes will just break down the door or blast it off.

Out-of-Character Alert: The villain has captured someone and sends a message in their name to their family or friends. However, something in the message tips off the Hero that something isn't right.

Out of Sight, Out of Mind: Where something is "destroyed" or otherwise dealt with by just throwing it off-screen.

Outrun the Fireball: Where a character survives a fireball by avoiding the actual fire, regardless of the hot air that should have flash fried them.

Outside Ride: Where somebody rides on the top or side of a moving vehicle.

Paper-Thin Disguise: An extremely transparent disguise that anybody in their right mind could see through, yet the on-screen characters can't.

Passing the Torch: When the experienced or elder Hero is ready to retire, and thus bestows the title or responsibilities of being a Hero on another.

Paying for the Action Scene: A character gets into a fight in a private establishment and pays for the mess they created.

Percussive Prevention: Stopping someone from doing something stupid by knocking them out and then doing it yourself.

Pin-Pulling Teeth: Using your mouth/teeth to pull the pin on a grenade before you throw it. Often because your other hand is unusable, or it's just bad-ass.

Pit Trap: A hole in the ground that's covered up, so as to blend in with the surrounding terrain.

Powder Trail: A trail of gunpowder left on the ground as a makeshift fuse to blow up stuff.

Plummet Perception: When a Hero sees or notices something that is useful later, only because they happen to be falling at the time.

Precarious Ledge: When a Hero has no choice but to navigate a dangerous ledge.

Precious, Precious Car: A jerk has a car which they love and absolutely refuses to let anyone touch. It will either be stolen, destroyed, or both.

Prisoners with Jobs are Loose: When "prisoners with jobs" are freed during a large battle, to either aid the heroes directly or increase confusion in the ranks of the enemies.

Punch! Punch! Punch! Uh-oh...: In a fistfight, one character delivers a set of rapid-fire punches into the other one's gut, only to have them smile and start delivering serious violence.

Punched Across the Room: When someone takes a hit or is thrown and flies across the room, hits a wall, and then falls to the ground, often with only a superficial wound to show for it.

Quicksand Sucks: Any sort of environmental hazard where falling and being engulfed or covered would be deadly.

Reed Snorkel: Plucking a hollow reed and using it to breathe while underwater.

Removing the Earpiece: When an agent or operative removes their communication earpiece to disobey an order, go rogue, or say something "off the record."

Rising Water, Rising Tension: Rising flood waters create new hazards and a sense of urgency.

Road Sign Reversal: A villain or prankster mucks things up by flipping road signs so they point in the wrong direction.

Rooftop Confrontation: A fight on a rooftop, which often ends with someone falling.

Rope Bridge: If you see one, you know one side is going to have the ropes cut, or the planks are going to fall down.

Saw It in a Movie Once: Where a character pulls off something they realistically shouldn't be able to, or even know how to do, and explains by saying, "I saw this in a movie once."

Scary Surprise Party: Something nasty happens to a character (kidnapped, in danger), but it turns out to be a surprise party.

The Scrounger: The person our Heroes turn to when they need supplies.

Secret Underground Passage: A hidden path, often located under old houses, or in bad guy lairs.

Shark Pool: A body of water filled with any variety of unpleasant creatures, such as alligators, killer jellyfish, piranhas, or sharks.

Sheep in Wolf's Clothing: Someone who's part-way transforming into a monster/zombie/robot/whatever manages to resist the change, keep their will, and help their human friends.

Shoot the Fuel Tank: Shooting a fuel tank makes it explode.

Shoot the Rope: When a character is about to be hanged, the cavalry will come to the rescue and shoot the rope.

Shooting Something So it Blows Up: When you shoot something so that it blows up, whether it should be able to explode or not.

Silent Running Mode: The crew of a ship have to be as quiet as possible so enemy noise detection won't pick them up.

Skeleton Key: A key that will open any door or lock. Often shaped like a skeleton.

Skeleton Key Credit Card: You can open any locked door by taking out a credit card and sliding into the door jamb, popping the latch.

Sky Heist: Either using a flying aircraft to steal something on the ground, or a heist that takes place on a flying vehicle.

Slipped the Ropes: A tied up character reveals that he or she slipped their bonds earlier and waited till this moment to reveal it, for some reason.

Smoke Out: Drop a smoke bomb and slip away while everybody's coughing.

Soft Glass: When you throw yourself through a pane of glass, shattering it, you can get right up and keep going.

Stab the Scorpion: A lethal attack that initially appears to be meant for the Hero is instead meant for something out-of-frame that was trying to kill them.

Stealth Hi/Bye: When a character either suddenly appears or disappears in a scene.

Super Window Jump: To get to or from the scene in a hurry, just jump through a window.

Superhero Landing: Landing in a half-crouch, with one knee and one hand on the ground.

Supernatural Martial Arts: Any version of a hero or villain being able to do things beyond normal human limits through their martial arts training.

Super Power Origin Montage: A Montage (either in real time or flashback) detailing how a Superhero gained their powers (and/or learned about the power and responsibility of being a Superhero).

Sword and Gun: A character simultaneously wielding a gun in one hand and a sword in another, or another combination of projectile and melee weapons.

Tactical Overlay: A real-time computer map is shown with the positions of military units (often in infrared) moving to engage with an enemy force.

Take Up My Sword: The hero dies, and a new hero takes up the old hero's mission.

Taking Over the Town: Villains cut a town off from the outside world so they can use it for their own nefarious purposes.

That's Bait: The BBEG or their minions use a hostage or the McGuffin to lure the Heroes into a trap. Often, at least one hero will recognize it but will still be compelled to enter the trap.

The Anticipator: When someone's arrival is supposed to be a secret, this character is always waiting for them. They can sense others' presence and are prepared for every contingency, because they've already anticipated every possible move.

The Big Inspirational Speech: When a hero rallies everyone to renew the fight by giving an impromptu, but perfect, inspiring speech.

The Cavalry Arrives Late: The cavalry arrives to offer aid, but only after the Heroes have already saved the day. Still, it's good for a ride back home.

The Idol's Blessing: Before the hero can truly win, they must receive the full support of the person they admire most.

The Radio Dies First: When in a crisis situation and having a radio would be way too easy a way to solve the problem, then the radio is the first (and maybe only) piece of equipment that will not work.

This Way to Certain Death: A dangerous area is marked by the corpses or bones of those who previously entered it.

Those Were Only Their Scouts: An initial victory over the enemy followed by the chilling realization that those were only the first wave and, possibly, weakest of the enemies.

Time Bomb: A character must succeed within a time limit, or bad things will happen.

Tired of Running: I've had it with being pursued. It's time to kick some ass!

Train Escape: A train is used to end a chase, either by crossing the tracks just in time ahead of it or by hopping aboard just as it departs.

Train-top Battle: A battle atop a moving train (or any moving vehicle).

Trick-and-Follow Ploy: Where you find out the location of the enemy's secret base by tricking an ally of theirs to go there and deliver some kind of communication.

Trojan Horse: When something dangerous is hidden inside another object that is able to get inside an otherwise secure location.

Trojan Prisoner: The Heroes pose as guards transporting a prisoner.

Troll Bridge: The Heroes must outwit someone guarding a bridge in order to cross.

Tuck and Cover: Saving someone else from an explosion by leaping on them and taking the blast for them.

Underside Ride: A character hitches a ride underneath a vehicle.

Unfeasible Vehicle: When a Hero is forced to use a less-than-desirable vehicle for a chase.

Unflinching Faith in the Brakes: A character standing in the path of something dangerous will unflinchingly stand there, knowing whatever it is will stop just inches from them.

Universal Driver's License: The hero will know, or will quickly figure out, how to drive or operate any vehicle, regardless of its general control scheme.

Unlimited Ammo: When a weapon that uses and needs ammo never needs to be reloaded, despite being used well beyond the normal capacity for that weapon.

Unstoppable Rage: When the Hero gets utterly furious and uses that rage to completely own the bad guys.

Unwilling Suspension: A character is tied up and suspended from the ceiling, often upside down.

Vapor Trail: A Hero or villain uses the gas spilling out of a vehicle's gas tank to ignite a trail back to the vehicle and destroy it.

Vertical Kidnapping: A character is kidnapped by someone from above them.

Villain's Throne: Hero walks into a dark room, turns on a light, and there's the villain, quietly waiting in his huge, dramatic chair.

Wait, What's This?: A character is looking at a photo that appears insignificant or unimportant at first, before then looking closer and finding an element that provides a critical clue.

Walking From an Explosion: When the Hero casually walks towards the camera and something erupts in a fiery explosion behind them, and they don't turn back or react in any way.

Walk the Plank: When a hero or ally is bound and forced to walk to their doom, often into deep, perhaps shark infested, water.

Water Wake-Up: A hero is awakened by a bucket of water or similar ignominious means, often after being captured, but occasionally as part of 'getting the team together.'

Weaponized Car: When a vehicle was built to include hidden weapons that can help the Hero or villain out.

We Don't Have the Budget for That: Where something incredible happens just off screen and we only see it through our character's descriptions/reactions (and maybe some lights), because it was too expensive to actually create or film.

Well, That's a Cliffhanger: Someone is dangling off the edge of a cliff and faces certain death. Just as they begin to slip, a hero (often out of frame until that moment) grabs them.

Wrong Wire: You cut the wrong wire, and now the countdown's moving faster!

Xantos Gambit: A plan for which all foreseeable outcomes benefit the creator — including ones that appear to be failure on the surface.

Your Shoe is Untied: When a hero distracts an enemy by briefly turning their attention elsewhere, such as by saying, 'Your shoe is untied,' or throwing a rock down a hallway.

You're the Bait: When a Hero or Supporting Character is used as bait to draw out a BBEG or their minions.

The tropes used were heavily inspired by those listed on **http://TvTropes.org.** If you want to add your own favorites, you can find many more there!

EJECTION SEAT

110

FREQUENTLY USED TERMINOLOGY

Here are some terms, defined as they are used in *Action 12 Cinema*.

Achilles' Heel: An Achilles' Heel is a negative aspect of a Hero, which can get them into trouble or cause them to make a bad situation worse. These can be words, sentences, or phrases, such as, "Can't stand to be thought of as a coward," "Too dumb to know better," or, "Risk Taker." Players can Leverage their Achilles' Heel aspect to give themselves two bonus d12s in a Dice Pool, but for this roll each 1 counts as two Setbacks, and can't be re-rolled by Leveraging their Heroic Trait. This is the only way to roll more than five dice in a single Dice Pool.

Act: Play in *Action 12 Cinema* is broken down into Acts. Each Act has a standard number of Obstacles to be resolved during play. Each Act can have any number of Scenes that occur at any number of locations.

Active Player: Players take turns being the Active Player. When you are an Active Player, you are in control of the narrative, can add or change elements, and can describe what happens in whatever over-the-top action you want.

Agency: The control each player has over their Hero and how they are portrayed within the fiction. No player may dictate the actions or portrayal of another player's Hero without their consent.

Attribute: Each Hero has four Attributes - Brains, Brawn, Charm, and Moxie - which help define how they interact with the story mechanically. Each Attribute is rated as either +0, +1 or +2. When using a given Attribute, the player adds a number of d12s to their Dice Pool equal to that Attribute's rating

BBEG: Shorthand for the main antagonist in a film; i.e., The Big Bad Evil Guy/Girl/Person. This is the force behind everything the Heroes will face during the game.

Character Sheet: A physical or digital document that allows the player to record whatever details, notes, game statistics, and background information they need to reference for their Hero during a play session.

Climax: The culmination of the plot, where the Heroes face off against the BBEG in the final battle or otherwise have a chance to defeat or overcome the dangers presented in the plot. In ***Action 12 Cinema***, this refers to the Final Obstacle presented in Act Three.

Complete Success: When a Success reduces an Obstacle's value to 0, that Success is a Complete Success. Once each Obstacle in an Act has reached Complete Success, the Act is over.

Concluding Scenes: The narrative scenes at the end of the game, once the Final Success has been resolved. This is the portion where each player narrates their Hero's response to the end of the movie, and where each Hero's Personal Crisis can be resolved, if appropriate.

Core Values: The three elements of ***Action 12 Cinema*** that should always be followed.

1. Maintain the established fiction.
2. Respect the other players' agency.
3. The Active Player decides what happens; the dice determine when and if an Obstacle is resolved.

Critical Failure: A Dice Pool is a Critical Failure if it has more Setbacks than Successes. When this happens, you add 4 points of value back to whichever Obstacle the Active Player was engaged with. If adding 4 points back to an Obstacle would take it above its original starting value (6 for a Minor Obstacle or 12 for a normal Obstacle), then you introduce a new Minor Obstacle instead.

D12: Shorthand for a 12-sided polyhedral die. Many RPGs feature dice of various sizes and types. ***Action 12 Cinema*** only uses 12-sided dice.

Dice Pool: During their turn, the Active Player will build a Dice Pool of d12s. A Dice Pool always has at least one die, and can have a maximum of five dice, or seven dice if the player Leverages their Hero's Achilles' Heel. The results of rolling the Dice Pool determine the outcome of the Active Player's actions. Results can be Setbacks (1), Blanks (2-7), Successes (8-11), or Heroic Successes (12).

Era: This is the general time period for the setting of the movie in an ***Action 12 Cinema*** session, as well as the general time period for that movie's production; i.e, the Era for a Sci-Fi movie may be 2323, but the Era for its production might be the 1950s. If not specifically stated, assume the movie and production to both be set in the current Era.

Established Fiction: Anything about the game world or setting that is stated as true becomes true, and continues to be true unless changed by player consensus, due to safety tool use, or through the mechanics of the game, like when an Obstacle is resolved by a Dice Pool result.

Exploding Dice: When you get a Heroic Success, you may choose to reroll any 12 and add the new roll result to the Dice Pool. If the result of the new roll is also a 12, you may continue to roll, adding each new result to the Dice Pool, until a different result is rolled.

Facilitator: The player who helps guide all the players through the Pre-Production Phase of an *Action 12 Cinema* game.

Final Obstacle: The name of the Obstacle with a value of 12 introduced in the Final Showdown. All of the Minor Obstacles must be resolved before the players can apply Successes towards the Final Obstacle.

Final Showdown: The name used for Act Three in *Action 12 Cinema*'s Three-Act structure. This is the portion of the game when the Heroes finally get to confront the BBEG and bring the movie to its climactic conclusion.

Final Success: The resolution of the Final Obstacle. Once the players reach the Final Success, the game moves into the narrative Concluding Scenes

Genre: A style of film, which comes with its own associated themes, style, and tropes.

Healing: Healing is the act of removing Stress from a Hero's elements. One use of Healing can remove Stressed from two elements, or can reduce one element from Broken to Stressed. Healing occurs for each Hero between each Act. Healing can also occur if any Active Player rolls two Heroic Successes (12) in a single Dice Pool, and chooses to use them to buy a Healing for the Table, or if any player says or does something at any point that causes the Table to erupt into laughter, then all of the Heroes get a free Healing.

Hero: The characters that the players create are called Heroes, and are the way the players will most often engage with the narrative fiction of the game's story and world.

Heroic High Five: When you get a Heroic Success, you may choose to save, or "bank", the die instead of immediately rerolling it. You may use these banked dice on another Active Player's turn to add Successes to their Dice Pool, in the form of a Heroic High Five When you roll a Heroic High Five, any result of 1-11 is considered a Success, and a 12 is considered a Heroic Success, but the only Heroic Success bonus you can choose is Exploding Dice.

Heroic Success: When you roll a 12 in your Dice Pool, that result is a Heroic Success. It counts as two Successes, and allows you to gain an additional bonus, such as a Heroic High Five, Healing, or Exploding Dice.

Heroic Trait: A defining characteristic that makes a player's character a Hero and not a Supporting Character. These are usually inherent, positive traits, like, "A Protector of the Weak," "Can't Stand Bullies," "Keeps to His Code," or "Iron Will." These can be words, sentences, or phrases. Players may Leverage their Heroic Trait a limited number of times during the game to re-roll Dice Pool results.

Inciting Incident: The first big element of a movie that brings the Heroes into the story against the BBEG, their forces, or other elements of the story they will be facing. In game terms, the first Obstacle introduced in Act One is the Inciting Incident.

Incremental Success: If you roll a Dice Pool and have some Successes, but not enough to completely resolve the Obstacle, these are called Incremental Successes. They should be paired with a narration or description of the Obstacle in some way becoming easier or less dangerous, but not yet fully overcome.

Leverage/Leveraging: Leveraging is a mechanical term for choosing to use an element of the game to add d12s to roll in your Dice Pool, allow re-rolls, or otherwise alter your results as the Active Player. You can Leverage Attributes, Skills, Relationships, and Tropes, as well as your Heroic Trait and Achilles' Heel.

Lines & Veils: Lines & Veils refers to the Safety Tool, as collected by Robert Ian Shepard. Lines are elements chosen and defined by players that WILL NOT be used in a particular session of an RPG. Veils are elements chosen and defined by players that may be used under certain conditions, generally only by reference or inference.

Location: Places where the action of the movie takes place. Examples include the local mall, an abandoned sea-side mansion, cyber space, or a space station on the edge of a black hole.

Minor Obstacle: An Obstacle that begins with a value of 6 (instead of the normal 12). There are two Minor Obstacles used in Act Three. If a Critical Failure results in a new Obstacle being introduced during play, it would be a Minor Obstacle.

Obstacle: The challenges that the Heroes must overcome in each Act of the story are called Obstacles. By default, an Obstacle enters play with a value of 12. Each time the Active Player rolls a Dice Pool during their turn, any net value of Successes is subtracted from the value of the current Obstacle they are trying to overcome. Once an Obstacle has been reduced to 0 points or less, that Obstacle is considered to have been resolved.

Opening Credits Scene: The name used for the introductory scenes that happen before Act One in **Action 12 Cinema**'s Three-Act structure. This is the portion of the game where the Heroes first come together, and just before the Inciting Incident is introduced.

Personal Crisis: An element of a Hero that makes their life more complicated, and may be causing physical or emotional stress. This Personal Crisis can be overcome through mechanical means during the game, if a player chooses to engage with it. An Active Player may remove one die from their Dice Pool in an attempt to make progress towards resolving their Personal Crisis, making one point of progress if the result is an Incremental or Complete Success. If a Hero gets three points of progress, they are able to resolve their Personal Crisis during the Concluding Scenes.

Production Phase: The second phase of gameplay is the Production Phase. This occurs after the Pre-Production Phase, and is when all the players take turns as the Active Player as they try to overcome Obstacles and progress through the Three-Act structure of the movie.

Post-Credit Stinger: A short scene revealed during or after the closing credits, which often gives additional context to the preceding story or sets up a possible sequel to the story.

Pre-Production Phase: The first phase of gameplay, in which the game is set up. This is where players will make choices, along with rolling on some d12-based charts, to lay out the general structure of the movie they'll be playing through.

Production Sheet: A physical or digital document that is used to collect various information about the game and setting as it is created, so that each player has access to that information.

Random Tables: During the Pre-Production Phase of an *Action 12 Cinema* game, there are various tables that will provide random elements. By rolling one or more d12s and consulting the charts, story elements are added to the game, based on what was rolled. In all cases, these charts are for inspiration only, and never are restrictive.

Rating: This refers to the film rating of the movie in your session of *Action 12 Cinema*. By default, *Action 12 Cinema* games are rated PG-13.

Relationship: Relationships are the personal connections a Hero has to other characters, including other Heroes or Supporting Characters. A Relationship can be Leveraged to add a d12 to a Dice Pool, either because the other person is physically in the scene with the Active Player's Hero, or from an emotional boost if, for example, knowing their fate would be in jeopardy if the Hero fails.

Rising Action: Act Two in an *Action 12 Cinema* Three-Act structure. This is the portion of the movie where everything is getting even more dangerous, and that danger is represented by the introduction of two Obstacles.

Safety Tools: Mechanics that help ensure every player will be comfortable with any elements of the game. For *Action 12 Cinema*, I encourage the use of Lines & Veils and the X-Card.

Setback: Any 1s rolled during a Dice Pool are called Setbacks, and count against the total number of Successes when determining the net value of your Dice Pool. Additionally, any 1s must be accounted for by applying Stress to an element used to build that Dice Pool.

Skill: Each Hero has a number of Skills that detail their character's specialized training. Each Hero has a total of five slots they can use to define Skills. Two of these are rated at +2, and three are rated at +1. When using a Skill during their turn to build a Dice Pool, the Active Player will add a number of dice equal to that Skill's rating to their Dice Pool. Skills can be created during the Pre-Production Phase or during play.

Stress/Break: Stress is a representation of the injuries and fatigue suffered by a Hero during the course of the movie. A Hero's elements (Attributes, Skills, and Relationships) can become Stressed or Broken during play. An element which has been Stressed can still be used normally, but it becomes Broken if it is Stressed a second time. A Broken element can't be used to build a Dice Pool until the Hero receives Healing and repairs the element to the Stressed condition.

Success: A die result of 8, 9, 10 or 11 counts as a Success. 12s count as a Heroic Success (two successes). Each Success reduces the value of a current Obstacle by one.

Supporting Character: The non-Hero characters that the players create, either during the Pre-Production Phase or during play, that interact with the Heroes are called Supporting Characters.

Trope: Any commonplace, recognizable plot element, theme, or visual cue implicit in the action movie genre.

The Worst Possible Thing: An aspect of a Location that's created during the game as short-hand for what might go wrong at this Location to increase the drama or tension.

X-Card: The X-card is a safety tool developed by John Stavropoulos, where a physical sheet of paper with a large X is placed on the table during a session of an RPG. A player may touch or otherwise indicate they want to use the X-card at any time, and whatever is currently happening in the game will be changed or halted with no questions asked. It is used to help ensure player safety and comfort during a session.

ADDITIONAL RESOURCES

THE LANGUAGE OF FILM

One of the easiest ways to make sure your **Action 12 Cinema** experience feels like you're playing in an Action Movie is to use film language as you describe your actions and narrate the scenes. Whether you are working towards disarming a bomb or introducing the new Obstacle of an alien-infected zombie horde rushing toward our Hero's makeshift bunker, framing and describing scenes with common film language will help present the game in the best possible light.

Film is a primarily visual medium, and so much of the language of film is used to convey information to, or evoke emotion in, those seeing it. That's not really how RPGs work - and more so games like **Action 12 Cinema**, which don't use maps or minis - so it's somewhat counter-intuitive to rely on the language of film.

The goal is to capture the feeling that the players are living in the world of a movie, and taking a few extra moments to describe the scene, the setting, actions, and even intent in this way helps keep everyone in that world. If you're a fan of movies at all, you may already be familiar with the language of film, but I suggest you read This is How You Make a Movie by Tim Grierson to better understand things like transitions, camera angles, blocking, camera POV, and more terminology that can really help put you and the other players in the right mindset for **Action 12 Cinema**.

CHARACTER ARCHETYPES

Action movies, particularly the bad (but fun!) ones, are filled with broad and shallowly defined characters. If you need inspiration for your Hero, choose or randomly select one of these archetypes from the list below. There is no difference between them mechanically — these are just for if you need inspiration.

EXAMPLES OF CHARACTER ARCHETYPES

The Absent-Minded Professor

The Bad Boy/Girl

The Blind Seer

The Boy/Girl Next Door

The Child

The Chosen One

The Gentle Giant

The Gentleman

Thief

The Hotshot

The Hunter of Monsters

The Jock

The Kirk

The Loner

The Lovable Loser

The Lovable Rogue

The Mad Scientist

The McCoy

The Outlaw

The Outsider

The Peacemaker

The Pessimist

The Sane Person in an Insane World

The Spock

The Town Drunk

The Whiskey Priest

INSPIRATIONAL VIEWING FOR ACTION 12 CINEMA

Many of these are movies which I discovered at an early age, and I watched so many of them so many times. A few are from a bit later - mostly to try and fill out some of the lists which were pretty slight - and a few may not truly be 'B-grade' movies, but I think each of these films help encapsulate the type of movie experience I envision when I sit down to play **Action 12 Cinema**.

ACTION-ADVENTURE

Mad Max

Escape from New York

Commando

Allan Quartermain and the Lost City of Gold

Big Trouble in Little China

King Solomon's Mines

Remo Williams: The Adventure Begins

Romancing the Stone

Monster Squad

ACTION-COMEDY

Surf Ninjas

The Cannonball Run

Smokey and the Bandit

The Adventures of Buckaroo Banzai Across the 8th Dimension

The Golden Child

Doctor Detroit

Zorro, the Gay Blade

Spies Like Us

Army of Darkness

ACTION-FANTASY

Masters of the Universe
The Barbarians
Kull the Conqueror
Mazes and Monsters
Highlander
Dungeons & Dragons
Hell Comes to Frogtown
Time Bandits
The Beastmaster
The Dark Crystal
Ladyhawke
Legend
Labyrinth

ACTION - HORROR

The Thing
C.H.U.D.
The Stuff
Piranha
Humanoids from the Deep
THEM!
The Blob (1988)
It's Alive
Phantasm
Q
Swamp Thing
Fright Night
They Live

ACTION - MARTIAL ARTS

Bloodsport
Marked For Death
Hard Target
Cyborg
Showdown in Little Tokyo
Enter the Ninja
American Ninja
Gymkata
The Last Dragon
Best of the Best

ACTION - SCI-FI

Universal Soldier
Face/Off
The Last Starfighter
I Come in Peace
Flash Gordon
The Running Man
Alien Nation
D.A.R.Y.L.
Enemy Mine
Explorers
Flight of the Navigator
Robinson Crusoe on Mars

ACTION - SUPERHERO

The Phantom
The Shadow
Dark Man
Spider-Man (1977)

ACTION - THRILLER

Invasion U.S.A.
The Punisher (1989)
Con Air
Firestarter
Iron Eagle
Lethal Weapon
Road House

ACTION - WESTERN

Young Guns
Young Guns II
Tombstone
The Quick and the Dead
The Magnificent 7 (2016)

THE 7 MOVIE PLOTS

When organizing your thoughts on the plot, use the descriptions below of The 7 Movie Plots as guidelines.

OVERCOMING THE MONSTER

The protagonist sets out to defeat an antagonistic force (often evil) which threatens the protagonist and/or protagonist's homeland.

RAGS TO RICHES

The poor protagonist acquires power, wealth, and/or a mate, loses it all, and gains it back, growing as a person as a result.

THE QUEST

The protagonist and their companions set out to acquire an important object or get to a location. They face temptations and other obstacles along the way.

VOYAGE AND RETURN

The protagonist goes to a strange land and, after overcoming the threats it poses or learning important lessons unique to that location, they return with experience.

COMEDY

Light and humorous character with a happy or cheerful ending; a dramatic work in which the central motif is the triumph over adverse circumstance, resulting in a successful or happy conclusion.

TRAGEDY

The protagonist is a hero with a major character flaw or great mistake, which is ultimately their undoing. Their unfortunate end evokes pity at their folly and the fall of a fundamentally good character.

REBIRTH

An event forces the main character to change their ways, and often become a better individual.

WHERE TO FIND ACTION 12 CINEMA

PODCASTS

Available through the website links below and anywhere you can find podcasts.

TABLETOP JOURNEYS - FIELD TRIP

Episodes 1-4
https://ttjourneys.com/archives/series/action-12-cinema

THE RPG ACADEMY

The Pre-Production Phase
https://therpgacademy.com/tsa-action-12-cinema-ep1/

Act One
https://therpgacademy.com/tsa-action-12-cinema-ep2/

Act Two
https://therpgacademy.com/tsa-action-12-cinema-ep3/

Act Three & Wrap Up
https://therpgacademy.com/tsa-action-12-cinema-ep4/

YOUTUBE

THE RPG ACADEMY

https://bit.ly/RPGAA12C

ROOK & RASP

https://bit.ly/RnRA12C

ROLL FOR FELICITY

https://bit.ly/R4FA12C

WANDERER'S HAVEN PUBLICATIONS

https://bit.ly/WHPA12C